The Streets Will Never Close

K'ajji

Lock Down Publications and Ca$h
Presents
The Streets Will Never Close

A Novel by *K'ajji*

K'ajji

Lock Down Publications
P.O. Box 944
Stockbridge, Ga 30281
www.lockdownpublications.com

Copyright 2020 K'ajji
The Streets Will Never Close

First Edition October 2020
Printed in the United States of America

Lock Down Publications
Like our page on Facebook: Lock Down Publications @
www.facebook.com/lockdownpublications.ldp
Cover design and layout by: **Dynasty Cover Me**
Book interior design by: **Shawn Walker**
Edited by: **Lashonda Johnson**

Stay Connected with Us!

Text **LOCKDOWN** to 22828 to stay up-to-date with new releases, sneak peaks, contests and more...

Thank you!

Submission Guideline.

Submit the first three chapters of your completed manuscript to ldpsubmissions@gmail.com, subject line: Your book's title. The manuscript must be in a .doc file and sent as an attachment. Document should be in Times New Roman, double spaced and in size 12 font. Also, provide your synopsis and full contact information. If sending multiple submissions, they must each be in a separate email.

Have a story but no way to send it electronically? You can still submit to LDP/Ca$h Presents. Send in the first three chapters, written or typed, of your completed manuscript to:

LDP: Submissions Dept
P.O. Box 944
Stockbridge, Ga 30281

DO NOT send original manuscript. Must be a duplicate.

Provide your synopsis and a cover letter containing your full contact information.

Thanks for considering LDP and Ca$h Presents.

Acknowledgments

CA$H and LDP, thank you for shining a light into the abyss. To all my brothers and sisters of the struggle. Together, nothing can stop us. As Kobe gave it to us on the court, Pac gave us the inspiration through his music. Chadwick gave us a vision as to what it should look like on screen as T'Challa. ...Throw that W across y'all chest in honor of those who've received their Wings and risen to the Heavens. Keep it there in appreciation of the hearts of our Women. For our Warriors on the front line all over the planet Warring to show the World that We matter! Hope, dream and believe! I'm wit'chu. To everybody out there excepting my calls and looking out for me through these dark times. You know who you are. Thank you for all your support. I love you. Q-Mac you know what it is. Where would I be without you? Granny, Momma, Tee-Tee, Cas! Just hold on. ...I'm comin'.

Message from The Author

Although this book has taken flight from behind these walls, I thank GOD. Without you, there is no me. I know it is not by my own strength that I am still strong. I dedicate this book to my two aunties we lost during its development. Lue and Cyn, I still can't believe you're gone. Just know that we miss you and we love you. To my family, my granny, my mother, Tee-Tee, and my son! You all keep me breathing in the *belly of the beast*. They've got me trapped. God willing, I'll make it home. Understand that *love* is an action word. You all already know. The biggest thanks go to Ms. Shaquan Riley. Your support throughout this journey is beyond measure. I love you!

To Johari, Kech, Olivia, Tykia, Cali Ebb, thank you all for being here. To my sisters, Squeek, Punkin, Trena, and Char —— Reez, keep a hawk ready, bruh. To my brothers, Rick, LilKeith, Kug, Loyal, G-One, Big Boobie — Ain't shit changed. Davon Mooky Malcolm, O.B. McMillan. To Deontrae Mayfield and Marcus D-Weapon Webb, thank you for your guidance and inspiration over the years. Deadly, you already know! Forever Music Man! Band Camp! Let's go! To the hood, I love you. If I ain't say it, you wouldn't know it. To my editing team at Full House Typing & Editing, I thank you from the bottom of my heart.

We've lost so many. R.I.P.: Bird, Bookie, J.B. Bump, Awesome, Terry T.P. Patton, LaZahn Tyson II Wright, Dre King, Jason Barnes, B.D., Dez, Pache, Nu-Nu, Nikki, Ki-KiTurner, Tina, Tony Rhone, Tony Stronge, D-2, Fatz, Tony Jenkins, Terry Barber, Q-Tip, Kaboo, Shooby, Squirt, Bout It B, Macho, Juicy *male, and female*. Danisha Yarbrough, I met an angel here on earth. Rest in peace, Queen. Autumn Ford, we miss you. Meka of Minnesota's R.A.N. Tecil Petty, Mama Jujee, Mama G, Destiny Davis, Cierra McGee, Frank Davis, Donya, rest in peace, baby. Last but not least, my nigga, Black.

To Chavet, Jymini, Ashley, and Essence! Your beauty speaks for itself gotta love you for simply being yourselves. Thank you! 12th our city lost something special in Sharnetta Falon, I can't imagine. Now Jamie, Mike Lawry, P.I. congrats on all you've accomplished. G, Anony...I love you! Greats study the greats! With that being said, CA$H! To the entire LDP team, you're blessed in this! Mo Dupe! Thank you! To my brothers down in Memphis: Dash, Deejay, Tee, and R.P. J-Little and Torey, what up? To my extended family down in the Mil. To the Hayes and the Phillups family! Clark St. what up? Moo, Doe, Sheeba, Tasha, Nikki, and Kebba Ke-ma R.I.P., Sporty, get it together, my nigga. You were one of the smartest dudes I'd ever met. To all the mothers that helped raise me, Rosie, Theresa, Delestine, Carol Bostick, Gloria, and Tip, I'll never forget. Young Dae'Jaun stay pure. Stay focused. Be king, keep praying. Your dad.

K'ajji

Prologue

Hood copped a crib for herself over on North 20th. She was still in a predominately black neighborhood. The only difference was that all the residents surrounding her were old. Hell, you rarely saw any of them at all unless they were outside in the summer, working in their gardens. But it was now winter and cold as a bitch! They were nowhere in sight.

We officially had a new hangout. Hood's shit was dope. She had wall-to-wall white carpet which made your feet feel as if though you were walking on cotton. There was Italian furniture in cream leather to match. Her entertainment center and 4500-gallon fish tank were my favorites.

The fish tank contained aquarium rock-sand, a *do not enter* sign, a shit-eater, and her two sharks. She took it back to Africa with her decorating scheme. She had everything from tribal masks, pictures, African vases, and wicker to really emphasize what she was trying to do. There were plants everywhere. Shit, she had all of us ready to do the damn thang. But, as she explained, we had to stay *incognito*.

Although her crib was for all of us, I can't front, I was jealous. We were all sitting in her living room on her soft leather, smoking good-good, and sipping my favorite wine. Can you say, Moscato? We had a few joints in rotation and I was high as shit! As we waited for the details on this next lick, we were taking votes. Everybody was on deck except Cyn, and I didn't like it one bit.

"Lue! Lue! You know you hear me, bitch! Damn, is you even here? Snap out of it," Mula said, snapping her fingers.

"You just gon' hold the bottle?" I said, "I'm empty, hit me up!"

"Oh, my bad, girl. This song had my ass somewhere else."

The song, *Let's Chill* by *Guy*, was playing softly in the background. I leaned forward to fill her glass but Hood put her hand over the top of it.

"Uh-uh, Lue," she said. "Hold up before you pour her ass another one. Mu, what's your decision on the count of Sherrice? Is Cyn in or is she out?"

"She's out! Now pour up," Mula said.

"A'ight, I guess that settles it. She out on this one," Hood replied.

"Hmph!" I huffed and crossed my arms.

"A'ight, y'all, this what we gon' do," Hood said, looking around the room at us.

"Damn, bitch, pass the weed! You hoggin' the shit," Sweets said, reaching for the joint.

Hood smacked her fingers. We all laughed. "Nah, here, my bad." Then she finally passed the *J*.

"I still don't see why Cyn ain't comin'," I said. "You hoes—"

"You hoes, what?" Hood griped. "We already voted on the shit. Y'all lost three-to-two! Damn, stop carryin' that shit. She's out end of discussion. Now listen—Lue, you listening?"

"Yeah, sis, I'm listening."

"A'ight," Hood continued. "Even though Atkinson Goldie went missin', his man and 'nem ain't missed a beat. Them nigga's still over there catchin' good paper and we going to get it."

"Bri, you used to fuck wit' Ready," Mula said. "You sure you good on this?"

"Bitch please don t ever question my P.Y.T. Let's go get this money." Bri blew out her smoke and said, "Sweets used to fuck wit T-Dog. I don't see nobody questionin' her."

"Well, excuse me, bitch. Damn, I wasn't questioning yo' touch, I was just askin'," Mu said, rollin' her eyes.

"Me and that nigga been through when I caught 'em wit that hoe, Tameera, off 31st," Bri said.

"So, you'll pop 'em?" Sweets asked.

"Wit' no hesitation and no regret. Damn, you questioning me, too?"

"Nah, we just gotta know. I mean, him bein' yo' first and all."

"Shit, you think? That gives me all the more reason. The nigga burnt me, remember?"

"Hell yeah, I remember!" Hood replied. "You was talkin' about killin' his ass back then. Was you serious?"

"I dunno, I was only thirteen. But I'm serious now. Can we get back to the money, please? Y'all trippin', if it comes to it, I'll kill 'em, a'ight? Now next. What we gon' do?"

"Daaammnn, you was thirteen?" I said. I hadn't heard that story.

"Not now, Lue," Bri said, wavin' me off.

I sucked my teeth. "Later then, bitch," I said. "Don't be mad at me. I ain't the one burnt chu." I smiled and she rolled her eyes.

"It's short notice but bro 'nem put me up on these niggaz last night," Hood said. "Bri, you down to play with Ready for a few days?"

"Damn, me again! I knew this shit was comin' when you mentioned dem niggas." Bri looked bitter, takin' a sip of her drink. "Shit, I need a personal joint now. Shit!"

"Bri, don't even trip, boo-boo. If you going in, I'm wit' chu." Sweets hit the weed. "I owe you that much. I'm the reason you met the nigga so—" She blew out her smoke. "I got T-Dog, he been dyin' to get some more of dis pussy."

"Watchu say, Bri?" Hood asked.

"I'm in," Bri replied.

"Y'all know bro 'nem used to get money wit' them niggaz, right?" Hood said.

K'ajji

THE PAST...

K'ajji

Chapter 1

2-Hood

Where I'm From

A lot of people don't know where we're originally from. I'm from what the Mil niggas and bitches call, *Dime Bag*. To me, the name seems to fit the murky, unforgiving hood with preciseness. It's a cortex, it's a part of me that will never leave. See, I was never blindfolded to the ominous ways of this world. Nah, I saw it as it was: assault, robbery, rape, drugs, and prostitution. I took it all in at an incredibly young age.

My mother was Niecy Fields. The streets knew her as *Intimate*. She was the better half of one of the many street kings out there. Back when my mom was fourteen, she met and fell head-over-hills in love with a nigga named Corteague Phillups. In the streets, he was referred to as Atkinson Teague, but she simply called him Teague. He was a young up-and-coming street hustler trying to make a name for himself. He was seventeen when he and mom met. He stood 6'1' and was black as oil with a pearly white smile. She'd actually met him one night she and her four friends, Yana, Trina, Iris, and Mahalia decided to attend a house party over on Locust.

It was the day her life changed forever. For a time, she and Teague were inseparable. But that, too, would change.
A year later, at fifteen, she gave birth to my twin brothers who arrived just minutes apart. She had no choice but to drop out of school and do her best to raise her babies. However, the WIC checks and food stamps fell short of their needs. She needed more than government assistance. Growing up her father was never around, so all she had was her mother. But with six younger siblings, there wasn't much her poor mother could contribute because she, too, depended on welfare.

Teague came around with his charm and finally convinced her to move out of my granny's house and into an apartment with him on Atkinson. Things were good between them for the first couple of months or so. But, as Teague's clientele grew, so did his head. Crack hadn't really hit the scene, yet. What some called, *H* and others called *Junk, Smack, Skag,* or *Black Tar,* in the streets, Heroin was the fiend's drug of choice. It didn't take Teague long to rise to the top of his game. His strategy was different than most ruffians his age. Instead of competing in the trade, he had another plan.

He began murdering anyone and anything which stood in the way of that ol' mighty dollar. If he thought you were getting too much money, he and his crew would rob you, simple as that. Escaping with your life was something most never saw, although he allowed some to breathe on. He started teaching his sons the game early on. Teague felt experience was life's best teacher.

So, by the time the twins were three, on several occasions, they'd already witnessed what the world had deemed the most depraved and vilest act against humanity: *Murder.* Teague's team sold dime bags. It's really how the hood earned its title, except the hundred-block. The shit was moving so fast that before he knew it, the highly addictive opioid had made him rich. In no time he was worth a few million. The game had been good to him. His product was known to hold five or six. This meant it could be multiplied five or six times its original amount.

It brought niggaz from all over to shop with them. Money wasn't a thang. He splurged on my momma and the others constantly. He took her on trips all around the world Paris, Italy, Germany, you name it, they'd gone there. She wanted to marry him very badly. Years went by as she patiently waited on the day he would ask her, and her dreams would come true. But that day never came. In fact, the more his money grew, the more estranged he became.

Soon, she felt she no longer knew this person she once loved more than herself. There were countless miserable nights she spent alone, crying, and wondering if he was even alive. He would sometimes disappear for weeks at a time.

My mother found herself calling his longtime friend, Tony, asking him about Teague's whereabouts. She knew if she ever needed anything, Tony was always there for her.

One year the streets were on fire and there was talk of a federal investigation. Bodies were dropping all over the city; reportedly most were from Heroin overdoses. Niggas were being greedy and hitting the raw with shit like Oxycodone, Percodan, Percocet, Tylox, and Fentanyl. I guess they were trying to quadruple some shit. Being naive, my momma thought Teague would see it was time to leave the game alone. She said he slowed down but he didn't stop. He seemed to be on top of the world. Rumor had it he was scared to put his money in the bank. So, he had *Glad* garbage bags filled with money and stored at different locations throughout the city. He'd bought dozens of cars: Big 'Lacs, Benzes, and he'd even gone so far as to cop a Maserati just to flaunt his wealth. He owned houses, bars, and a few dealerships. He had women in all shapes, sizes, and colors. He didn't hide it from my momma. She knew but refused to leave him.

K'ajji

Chapter 2

Betrayal

Shit hit the fan one summer night Teague came home early, and unexpectedly. He walked in to find his so-called best friend Grip, crashing my momma from the back. Hearing her moans and screams of passion as she called out another man's name pushed him over the edge.

Teague dragged Grip outside while he was still butt-ass naked and blew his brains out. Everybody on the block saw the shit. He didn't run, Teague leaned against his Corvette, lit a cigarette, and had a full conversation with Grip Harden's lifeless corpse.

"Nigga, what the fuck you doin' in my house?" he shouted. "Oh-hoo! You was fuckin' my bitch! You was fuckin' mine, Grip? Look at cha. Answer me dis! Was the pussy good, nigga? Ha-haaa!" He laughed, gun still in his hand as he took a puff from his Kool cigarette. He blew the smoke out and said, "Whatchu say? I can't hear you."

My momma was on the porch screaming, "Teeeague, I'm sorry!"

Teague was still talking to Grip. He heard her but never even looked in her direction. He said, "Huh? You think—you think I should kill her?" He pointed the gun at the porch where my momma was curled into the fetal position, still sobbing. Teague still couldn't or didn't care to look at her. "Nah, I think I got the right one." He took another hit of his square and blew out its toxins. "I came up wit' chu, Grip. I broke bread wit' chu, nigga." As he looked down at Grip, Teague never saw the police pull up.

Police cars pulled up from both directions onto the sidewalk. They jumped out with their guns drawn.

"Freezeee!" they yelled. Teague turned full circle, peeping his surroundings. "I said freeze goddammit! Drop the gun!"

He dropped the gun and smiled, it was over for him. The local authorities had patiently waited for him to fuck up, and he did. As

21

the officers cuffed him and walked him to the squad car, he looked at mom and said, "Intimate! Make sure you bring my boys to see me, bitch!"

Then he began yelling, "Moo-Moo! Doe-Doe! Moo-Moo! Doe-Doe!" he yelled their names in hopes of seeing them once more before he was taken into custody, but my mom told him they were asleep.

***

A month later my momma found out she was pregnant with me. She was devastated because she didn't know who the actual father was. However, my birth said a million words. Mom wasn't dark like Teague and the twins. But she wasn't considered light-skinned either. She had this reddish-brown color to her skin tone, sort of like coffee grinds. Me, I came out light as the sun. I was a healthy seven pounds and two ounces. She'd finally given birth to the little girl she always wanted. It was clear I was Grip's seed, but she gave me Teague's last name anyway. Although I always thought he hated seeing me, my mother used to take us to Oxford, Wisconsin to see him all the time.

Teague was doing Fed time. See, not only did they charge and convict him of the murder of his best friend, but while fighting the case, a 52-count indictment was handed down against him. They gave my brothers' daddy four life sentences. They hit him with everything from murder, kidnapping, racketeering, conspiracy, money laundering, and delivery of more than 10,000 grams of an uncontrolled substance. They tried to indict him for the 19 bodies that dropped dead six months before his incarceration as well. Eventually, the U.S. Attorney had to drop those counts because they had no direct links between Teague and all the deceased.

Then out of the blue, the unthinkable happened. My momma died of an overdose when I was nine years old. The medical examiner who performed her autopsy said her death was caused by a concoction of alcohol and Heroin found in her system. I couldn't believe she was gone. I couldn't believe God took her from us, my beautiful mother. To me, she was the best mother in the world. I knew she had a drink on occasion, but Heroin? That was a shock to us all. My mother never used drugs, ever! My brothers think it was a guilt trip regarding what she'd done to their father. I knew she'd only done what she did to get back at him for all the pain he'd caused her. I'm sure she never thought he'd be in prison fighting for his life. Surely, she never expected me. But she loved me, she loved us.

K'ajji

Chapter 3

On Our Own

After my mom passed, Doe and Moo tried looking after me the best they could, but they didn't know anything about raising kids. They were kids themselves, so we ended up moving in with Aunt Tip. I didn't know much about my father. My mother couldn't really tell me anything but his name and that he and Teague had grown up together. She didn't know anything about his family. Not only did they blame my mother for the destruction of an empire, but to them she was the cause of both men losing their lives.

Anyway, after the Feds seized everything, we were left to fend for ourselves. I had never met a soul from my father's side of the family. Then, when I was eleven, I found out I had a big sister. Her mother was struggling with addiction and couldn't take care of her so Aunt Tip took her in as well. Not only had Aunt Tip and her mom been old friends, but auntie felt it was the right thing to do. My sister's name was Shanbria but everyone called her Shebba. She was two years older than me, but we clicked hard!

She was a little bit taller than me, with the same skin complexion, curly hair, and chinky eyes. It was summer so we spent every waking hour together. We made a pact that we'd never let anything separate us! Not even death. My momma's best friends also stayed involved in our lives. Auntie Trina, Mahalia, and Yana were all blessed with daughters whom I grew up playing with. I was the oldest of all of them. Iris' daughter, Lue was too little so her momma wouldn't let her hang with Shebba, Pam, Bri, Karma, and me. Not at first.

However, once she turned seven, she allowed her to come around us more. My aunties Nikki and Kebba would invite us all to her crib and throw little sleepovers for us. We had pizza, popcorn, ice cream, and cupcakes. That shit was the bomb! Kebba would let us watch HBO all night until we fell asleep or until she thought we were asleep. However, on the low, sometimes she thought I was asleep, but I was up watching *Porkies* and *Sahara Heat* on *Friday Night After Dark* right with her ass.

I was fast as hell. But growing up I was a tomboy for real. I tried to do everything I saw my brothers do. That led me to hooping and a gang of other shit they exposed me to.

Chapter 4

I Want Some

Moo and Doe jumped off the porch early. Momma probably didn't know but their asses had been selling dope! I don't know what she thought Teague had been telling them when he'd ask us to take a trip to the bathroom or vending machines so he could *talk* to the boys. But his ass said something to them because my brothers knew too much, too young. One day when I was eight, I caught them bagging up in the basement. I was trying to sneak up on them so I flew down the basement stairs.

All I heard was, "Doe, oh shit! Here comes Tasha!"

Once I hit a few steps, he must have seen my lil' legs. Doe-Doe was trying to hide a plate full of rocks behind his back. My nosey ass was running from side to side, trying to see what he had.

"Whatcha got? Whatcha got, Doe? Let me see!" I yelled in a high-pitched voice.

"Shhh girl, this candy," he said.

"Well, I want some! Gimme, gimme, gimme or I'm tellin' momma!" I threatened with my hand out.

Moo put me in a headlock. "You gon' what? What I tell you about snitchin'?" he said, gritting his teeth.

"Let me go, Moo! Ahhh!" I screamed.

"Doe-Doe! Moo-Moo! What y'all doin' to my baby?" momma yelled from upstairs.

"Nothing Ma!" they both yelled in unison and Moo let me go.

"Give me some!" I said, rolling my neck and sticking my hand out again.

"Look!" Moo said, showing me the plate. "You can't eat none of this! This kinda candy ain't good for you. This for grown-ups."

"Well, why you got it then?" I asked out of curiosity.

"Cause we older than you. We just puttin' it in bags for when we get older," Moo said.

I knew they were lying, I just knew it.

"I tell you what," Doe said.

"What!" I folded my arms.

"I'll give you two dollars if you don't tell momma about this candy," he said.

"Two whole dollars?" I asked.

"Two big ones," Moo said, digging into his pocket. He pulled out a big-ass wad!

"Ooh, can I have three?" I asked.

"Hell naw," Moo said, handing me two dollars and stuffing his wad back into his pocket.

"Hold up," Doe said, looking at Moo sideways with his face screwed up. He pulled out his knot and said, "Make it five. Don't tell momma you seen no money either. If she asks you where you got it, tell her you been savin' up. A'ight?"

"A'ight," I said, stuffing the money in my pocket with a smile. Shit, after that, every time I caught their asses putting grown folks' candy in bags, I got paid. I didn't know where they were getting all that money, but I knew they were getting it.

Chapter 5

Moo and Doe

They say a childhood lasts 6,570 days. That might be true in some cases but not in most at least not where I 'm from. It seemed the majority of us were forced to grow up overnight. Personally, the only reason I think God made two of me was because He knew things would be twice as hard. There's this old saying which says, *"He never gives you more than you can handle."* Well, I wonder why it feels like we've been cursed since birth. Born two months premature, we weren't expected to live, but, against all odds, we did. Then we lost both of our parents.

Sunday 10:12 p.m.

At fourteen years young, Moo, Doe, T-Dog, and Ready posted up on 10th in A.T.K. grinding like they did every day when a swerve pulled up to the curb.

Ready said, "I got this one! I got this one!"

He and T-Dog raced toward the car, trying to bump each other out of the way. It was dope-fiend Lisa from around the corner. She'd spent a few hundred with Moo earlier that morning. He'd also tricked off a few bags, Lisa was cold!

He couldn't believe she was a smoker. The youngsters were at her window, yelling like stockbrokers while Moo and Doe played the back.

T-Dog yelled, "I got them hubbaz!"

Ready tried to outbid him, "I got them sacks for yo' back! Look, look, look, look," Ready said, holding out a hand full of boulders.

"Uh-uh, I wanna holla at twin!" Lisa said.

"Which one?" Doe asked, hearing the conversation.

"He knows who I 'm talkin' to. The one with the big dick!" she said.

Moo stepped forward as any hope for a lil' cash escaped his friend's mind. Their shoulders slouched as they cuffed their work and moped back to Doe's side. Moo jumped into the car and they pulled off. He came back a few minutes later, walking through the cut. He had a big smile on his face as he counted out the $75.00 Lisa had just spent.

"So, that's where you disappeared to this morning? Ha-haaa!" Ready said.

"Moo, we see yo' ass been trickin'. Ahhh—ha—haa!" Doe pointed, putting him on blast.

Everybody was laughing harder than a bitch! "The one with the big dick? Shit, we twins' but remember, you came out two minutes before me. That's proof I stay in the pussy longer, nigga!" Doe said, still laughing.

Moo smirked. "Yeah, a'ight. You got that one, lil' bro," he said, clutching his piece as Ready and T-Dog laughed even harder.

Moo raised his eyebrows and said, "You damn right I tricked! Lisa got a stupid ass and a fat pussy. And the head! Oh, my Goddd!" He stomped his feet. "Baby got skillzzz."

"Oh, shit, nigga let me find out that was yo' first piece of pussy!"

"First—*first piece of pussy?*" Moo looked around, mapping his escape route. "Nigga, you know I been fuckin' yo' sister!" he said.

The laughter from T-Dog stopped. Moo paused, T-Dog rushed him, trying to grab him. Moo took off running as Doe and Ready stood there cracking up.

"I'm just playin'! I'm just playin'!" Moo yelled with T-Dog hot on his tail.

***

It was a typical night out in the hood. The A.T.K. crew consisted of six lil' niggaz, the twins, Ready, T-Dog, Goldie, and J-Prince. They'd all grown up together on the block. At sixteen, Goldie was the oldest but he and Prince had to be in by 10 p.m. Cousins Ready and T-Dog mommas didn't give a fuck when they made it home. Sadly, all they were worried about was their next hit. They were chasing a feeling they'd never feel again—that first blast.

Doe and Moo had to be home by 10:30 p.m. because they all had school in the morning. But it looked like they were going to be late as usual. Tip was bound to get their asses. She was still letting them attend school at Parkman for the time being, but she'd already warned them that if they came home late one more time she was switching their asses to Malcolm X, especially since she lived on 3rd in Chambers, MX was their district. She'd already switched Tasha from Keefe Avenue to Palmer Elementary so that she and Sheeba could be together.

It was 11:10 p.m. when they walked through the door. Tip was waiting on them, too. They stopped at the door when they saw her. "Well, hell! If it ain't lil' nigga and his shadow even littler nigga?" she said calmly as she lounged in her La~Z-Boy recliner, watching Johnny Carson. "Well y'all's late, ain't cha? Come on in!"

Moo tried to say something. "Yeah, but—"

"But my ass, Moo! Don't make me get up. Gon' in there, wash y'all hands and eat. Y'all food on the stove. When y'all get done, take a shower and go to bed. I'm enrollin' y'all asses in Malcolm X in the mor—nin'."

"Aww! C'mon, Ms. Tip—"

"Aht, I don't wanna hear it. Gon' now!"

"Damn!" Moo uttered underneath his breath as they marched toward their bedroom.

"And Doe-Doe and Moo-Moo!" she called out to them.

"Huh?" They turned back to her.

"Come in this house late again, after 10:00 p.m. on a school night, I'ma do somethin' to ya. Understand?"

"Yes, ma'am," they said in unison.

The next day, just as she said, she enrolled them in Malcolm X. They were pissed! It was the middle of the school year. Therefore, being twins and *on the new*, everybody noticed their arrival. To their relief, they knew a couple of niggas off Chambers who went there as well.

Tank, O-Jilla and Phife were just a few. They happened to run into them at their lockers on the way to the second-hour class. Jilla was the first to accost them.

"Doe and Moo, what the fuck y'all Parkman-ass niggaz doin' here?"

"We got transferred this morning," Moo replied with dread. "What up with y'all?"

"Shit, about to go to this boring ass Science class and put up with Mr. Randall's shit," Tank replied.

"Where y'all headin'?" Jilla asked.

"I'm headin' to math," Doe replied.

"I got English," Moo said.

"What's up with the hoes?" Doe asked.

"Aw, it's plenty lil' bitches here. If you ain't seen nothin' you like yet, trust me, you will," Phife told him. "What hours you niggaz got lunch?"

"We got fourth hour," Doe replied. "What about y'all?"

"We'll see y'all there! We got our own table so just come holla!" Tank said as they strolled off.

"Yeah, we'll introduce y'all to a few pieces!" Phife hollered over his shoulder.

"A'ight, bet!" Doe hollered back and shut his locker. The bell rang. They were both late.

Though the homies from the hood were just as pissed about the switch as they were, over the next few months the twins started liking X more and more. Parkman had an after school program where you could go shoot pool, hoop, play video games, and get on the computer. But the ladies at Malcolm X had them intoxicated. They had a certain sexiness about them. Being a couple of new faces hadn't been as bad as they expected. In fact, it had worked in their favor. The honeys were giving them much attention and they loved every minute of it.

Moo had his eye on Destiny, a lil' chick off the Northside. She was a Phenomena people called them *Philos* for short. The Philos was a clique of girls she belonged to and all of them were bad. They were dark-chocolate, redbones, light-chocolate, and even white-chocolate if you wanted a mulatto. A nigga couldn't lose! Once Phife gave the introduction, he left the rest up to Moo.

"Yo, who that redbone over there?" Moo asked Phife as they sat at their table in the library one afternoon.

"Shit, which one?"

"The one with the blue Guess sweater on and the skirt?"

"Oh, that there is De-sti-nyy. She butter, ain't she?"

"Hell yeah, nigga," Moo whispered.

"Watch this. Yo', Destiny Philo!" Phife yelled.

The librarian shushed him.

"Dog, she smiled. I think she smiled at me." Moo was trippin'.

"Be cool," he told Moo. "Say, come talk to me for a minute!"

"Ooh shit, here she comes."

"Relax, nigga, I got you," Phife told Moo.

Destiny sashayed her way over to the table. "Hey Phife. What up?" she said, sexy as ever with a smile.

"I wanted to introduce you to my nigga, Moo," Phife told her. "He said he thinks you fly."

"Enough to hold up the sky." Moo stood to greet her with a handshake and a smile.

"Hey, Moo, nice to meet you," she replied, blushing as she shook his hand.

"Hey, how you doin'? Is Destiny Philo your real name?"

"No," she said. "But Destiny is, Philo, is my crew."

The bell rang.

"Des—Destiny, we out!" one of her girls whispered.

"A'ight y'all, I gotta go. See y'all later, 'kay?"

"For sure!" Moo yelled as she hurried to catch up with her friends.

The librarian scolded them. "Get out! This is a library, not a lunchroom. How dare you?" She was pissed.

"Come on, Moo. We out," Phife said. They got up and left.

Moo wanted Destiny badly, the only problem was, according to niggaz from 3 Chambers, she fucked with a nigga named Seneca off Clybourne. They said he was H.T.P. *Hill Top Posse.* The nigga didn't go to *X* he went to Jeneau. He was actually in high school. Moo started seeing him come pick up Destiny in a black Grand National and shit. She was high maintenance, he knew he'd have to push his hustle game to the limit before he even attempted to step to her. Then he came up with an idea that sounded genius to the crew.

Chapter 6

Let's Get It

It was time to hit A.T.K. like never before. Smack dead in the middle of the block was an apartment for rent. Moo convinced the gang to pitch in and rent it out. The only thing stopping them was their ages. But, with the help of one of Goldie's loyal customers, they got the place and opened up shop that same day. Dime bags were in full swing. Altogether, they were only copping 4 ½ ounces. But, with plans to buy a brick as their first mission, they tried to spend every hour they could pushing nothing but dimes. They came up with *four-for-twenty Tuesdays* which brought the fiends in droves.

T-Dog and Ready were the only two who could pull all-nighters during the week. It was good for business because the shop never closed except during school hours. Shit, that's if niggas went. Dog and Ready, seeing more money than they'd ever seen, started saying, *fuck school,* and began staying at the spot. They set it up where fiends would come through the alley, walk up to the crib, and tap on the back bedroom window. The number of times they tapped represented how many dimes they wanted. Once they handed them the money, they received the product.

All the customers saw was a hand but not who was serving them. They were running shit like a drive-thru window. After flipping the first 126 grits twice, they grabbed the nine-piece. They had the math mapped out and in no time their come-up was starting to show, and Destiny took notice. She couldn't help but see the fresh attire, bones, and the nuggets. Moo and Doe rocked shit well and to perfection. Now all they needed was a ride.

Shit was running smoothly until one-night T-Dog and Ready had to learn the hustlers creed the hard way. It was a Monday night and it had been fairly slow. The entire spot was empty except for a refrigerator, a stove in the kitchen, a couch, and a TV in the room they used to sell out of. T-Dog and Ready were rocking back and forth with their eyes glued to the screen as they waited to hear the next tap on the window for product.

Ready was like, "Nigga, I'm telling you now, you can't see me in this shit! Oh, here it come!" Deep into their game of Atari, they never knew what hit them.

Boom! The back door to the spot came crashing in. They heard footsteps, thinking it was the police.

"What tha—" Ready said as he leaned over the couch and looked towards the kitchen. All he saw were figures in all black with guns.

They rushed the back room screaming, "Get down! Get down! Get the fuck down!"

Within seconds three niggas in all black had them stretched out on the floor with guns to their heads. One of the masked men asked, "Where the money at, lil' niggas? I see the dope!"

They had a white bucket with dimes in it sitting next to the window. "In my pocket!" Ready said. "Don't shoot man. Take that shit!"

It was clear the voice Dog and Ready heard was the nigga in charge. He was the only one speaking for the time being.

"Roll yo' ass over, nigga," he said, kicking Ready in his side.

When he rolled over, they saw his pocket had the mumps. Two fat wads protruded from his jeans. The niggas damn near ripped his pockets off as they grabbed the money.

"Count that shit," the leader told his niggas. "Yo', turn yo' ass over! Whatchu got?" he asked as he kicked T-Dog in his ass.

"Nut—nuttin'," T-Dog replied, turning over with his eyes closed. He didn't have shit on him but two Charleston Chews. They could hear a fourth man searching the house as they laid on the floor.

"Is this it lil' muthafuckas? And y'all bet not lie! If you lie, and my man finds somethin' else, I'm blastin' y'all asses! Now, is this it?"

"Yeah, that's it!" T-Dog yelled. He just wanted the niggas gone.

"Niggas, flip the couch and shit! How much is that shit? Key, you find anything?"

Another voice said, "Damn nigga, fucks wrong with you? This three-thousand, six hundred, eighty dollars."

Then another voice in the distance said, "Nah, ain't shit out here. Let's go!"

"A'ight, nice doin' business with you, sweet ass niggas!"

The next day after school when the rest of the team fell through. T-Dog was there to break the news, Ready was gone. He went to holla at the nigga they were copping from to see if he had a connect on some pistols. Doe and Moo immediately headed back to Tip's crib to get the burners Teague had left stashed in the basement of the old crib. Back at the spot, the question was, how did niggas get past the first two doors? The screen door had cast-iron bars and was locked. Plus, the door they entered before they hit the kitchen door had a deadbolt on it.

The niggas had to have a key because neither door was damaged, and, the upstairs apartment was vacant. Goldie paced back and forth, trying to figure shit out as T—Dog, and Prince sat on the sofa.

"So, niggas got us, huh?" Goldie said. "Almost three thousand, seven hundred and fifty in cash and another three-thousand in dope."

"You ain't recognize nothin' particular about the niggas?"

"Nah, not really," Dog said. "Niggas was all in black. One had a shotgun and the other two had handguns. I closed my eyes, I ain't want 'em to have a reason to get to shootin'. I don't think the fourth dude even came back here."

"My question is, how the fuck the niggas get in the bottom doors?" Goldie said. "We the only ones with the keys."

T—Dog replied, "Aw yeah! Now that you said somethin', I remember the nigga callin' all the shots call one of the niggas, Key."

"Key, where do I know that name from?" Goldie said, rubbing his chin.

Ready ended up getting back before the twins. He had good news, Vell had a connect who would supply them with artillery which was clean and for the low. Once everybody in the crew was present, they sat down and discussed what T-Dog had mentioned earlier. But nobody seemed to know anybody by the name Key.

Goldie knew he'd heard the name before, but where? They sat and racked their brains for hours but came up with nothing.

Meanwhile, fiends were still coming and tapping on the window for work to no avail. Before they opened up again some changes had to be made. They came to an agreement on a few things. First things first, they had to secure the spot. They went and hollered at the *old head* from the block and bought everything the connect had on hand. Next, they got the locks changed and since Goldie was the oldest, he was the only one who would have a key. When Dog and Ready stayed the night, which had become the norm, there would be no more Pac Man or Space Invaders. While one worked, the other was to be on security.

Only when everybody was there and there was at least two people on security was the game to be played. They would switch off on security. The robbery was a minor setback. They still had enough to grab 18 ounces and Vell threw in 18 on consignment, so they were playing with the bird. They broke 18 ounces down into everything from dimes, dubs, 50 cent pieces, and 16ths. They broke the other 18 down into ounces, quarters, halves, and balls. The block was doing numbers. Then, two weeks later, Moo and Doe had finally stacked enough for a whip. They ended up buying a black Monte Carlo.

Both fell in love with it the moment they saw it. It was an '84 and everything was original inside and out. Although neither of them could barely drive, they were just in time for the 8th-grade dance. The twins and the niggas Tank, Phife, and Jilla were sitting in the cafeteria. They were trying to get Moo to make his move and ask Destiny to the dance. Although they knew nine times out of ten he was going to make a fool of himself, they still egged him on, trying to see if he would budge.

"Yeah, Moo, man. You been talking all that shit, nigga," Tank said. "There she go right there. I bet you won't go ask her to the dance, right now."

"Man, that nigga been sweatin' that girl ever since we got here," Doe said. "I don't know what the fuck he waitin' on. Brah, what up? I know you ain't scared?" He laughed.

"Hell nall, I ain't scared, nigga. I'ma ask her," Moo said. He was nervous, he rubbed his hands together as he glanced over at Destiny and her friends.

"Well, do it now, nigga! I dare you," Jilla said.

"Nigga, I triple dog dare you!" Phife said. "I bet five hunnid she says nall."

"Say no mo'," Moo replied.

He got up, turned his swag up a thousand, and strolled over to the table full of Philos. They were in the midst of one of their lil' girly conversations. But when Moo walked up all that ceased. They all stopped talking and stared at Moo. A few whispered to one another while others giggled.

"Hey, excuse me y'all," he said. "Destiny, I was wonderin' uh—if you had a date for the dance Friday?"

One of Destiny's friends laughed. "Ooh, Destiny, Seneca—" she started to say.

"Shut up, Myra!" Destiny checked her. "Ain't nobody talkin' to yo' ass anywayyys," she continued, rolling her eyes and turning her attention back to Moo. "No. As a matter of fact, I don't. I got a man, but he acts like he too good to show up at a middle school social event now that he's in high school. Are you askin' me to be your date?"

"Hell, yeah! I mean—yeah, yea—yes, I am. Will you be my date?" he asked her nervously.

"Sure," Destiny replied. "You can pick me up at six p.m. sharp in that car y'all think y'all been hiding around the corner every day. I'll write you and send you my address later. And, you bet not give it to nobody."

"I won't," Moo said with a smile. "A'ight, see you later." He was geeked.

He walked back to the table where the guys were with a big Eddie Murphy smile plastered across his face. He told Phife, "Geh my money, nigga!" Phife reached for his pocket but Moo said, "Not right now, nigga. Chill. I know you got it."

True to her word, Destiny wrote him a letter that contained her address and surprisingly, her phone number as well. She also wrote how she thought he was the cuter twin and how much she was look-ing forward to going to the dance with him. For Moo, Friday couldn't come fast enough.

Chapter 7

You Gon' Eat with Me

Teague

That week, I remember Aunt Tip packing us all in the car and going to see Teague. The Federal pen is a trip. The security is crazy tight. It always took us a good 45 minutes just to get in. It's so hard getting into the muthafucka I couldn't imagine a nigga trying to break out. They had all kinds of metal detectors and there were invisible stamps you could only see with a certain light. When we finally got in it was like we were visiting an entirely different person.

Gone was the man I knew growing up as a child. His long, wavy hair was now mostly gray and looked as white as snow. His flawless, chocolate skin had cracked. He was stressed and it showed. He'd been down for 10 long years and at 35 he looked twice his age. But, I could still see the fire of hope in his eyes. First, he greeted Tee-Tee with a strong hug, but his eyes never left the twins as he squeezed and hugged his sister tightly. It was as if he knew they were up to something.

They were growing and looking like him more and more every day.

"My boyz," he said as he hugged them with his massive arms.

"Sorry about y'all momma. Come give me a hug, Tasha," he said, looking over at me.

"Nope!" I said, folding my arms. "Nigga gon' try to hug me last."

He laughed. "Ha-ha, lil' girl y'all momma raised y'all in the hood. But yo' lil' ass just ghetto. Come here!" He snatched me off my feet and gave me the warmest hug I'd ever gotten. He put me down and looked at me. He extended his hand to me and I grabbed it.

"Look at you, all grown," he said. "You gotcha mother's eyes."

I said, "Emm-hmm!" I smiled, rolling my eyes and neck.

He smiled. "Come on over here and sit down. Let's get something to eat."

I was trying to act like I was mad at what he did to my daddy. I told him I wasn't hungry but he insisted, so I got louder. It was all for attention. Quiet as it was kept, I was jealous of his relationship with the twins.

"I said I ain't hungry!" I yelled.

"You gon' eat with me," he said, smiling and shit. The nigga knew he had charm.

"She sumthin' else, ain't she?" Aunt Tip told him.

"Emm-hmm," he replied. "She too hood, that's what I'ma start callin' her, too. Maybe she'll start actin' lady-like."

Somehow, he saw right through me. He knew I was frontin' and since it was my first time acting out in front of him, I guess he figured it was because of my momma. Or he very well could have assumed I'd heard about what went down between him and my pops. After all, in my opinion, we were old enough to know. If we weren't old enough to know, my momma sure didn't think so.

Plus, the twins and I used to sit up and listen to all the stories about Teague and my daddy over the loud, drunken card games Aunt Tip would have every weekend. Those niggas stayed in some shit. From what we heard, they started out as petty car thieves. Then they graduated to robbing gas stations and convenience stores. It grew from there to robbing niggas in the streets and selling dope. The rest was history, sex, money, and murder.

It's all a game, but whose? I know we all hate losing but somebody's got to. You'll always have a handful of niggas who will hate to see you winning, it's fucked up. Anyway, we ordered up some shit. We had pizza, chicken, chips, burgers, and all kinds of candy. Ooh, I had my favorite— microwave popcorn.

Teague was talking a foreign language to me. He was talking about something called an appeal. I also heard him say something about his lawyer needing twenty more thousand and Tee-Tee telling him she'd do what she could to help. He told her there were still niggas on the street who owed him money, and he wanted it. Moo and Doe listened intently, I thought they were going to say something but when they didn't, I did.

"Moo and Doe got money," I said, munching on my freshly popped popcorn. "They got candy for grown folk. They can help you, Teague."

Moo and Doe had gas faces. "Candy, what candy?" he said, looking at the twins.

Both of them gave me scolding looks. I knew I was going to get it. Ha-haa, yeah, I told on them. They told me not to tell momma and I didn't. Shit, I didn't know any better. I thought I was helping Teague, and I really just wanted to get in on the conversation.

"Tip, take Too Hood and y'all go grab us some more food or some more pop or somethin'. Give me a few minutes with the boyz," Teague said. I knew he'd heard about them coming home late. I was sure he'd heard they'd had to switch schools. But now I knew he had no idea they'd been hustling cocaine. Well, he knew now, me and my big-ass mouth. Maannn, those niggas hadn't given me any money for about a year!

K'ajji

Chapter 8

You Lil' Niggas Never Learn

Sen

The night of the eighth-grade dance finally arrived but it wasn't at all what Moo expected. When he pulled up on 36th in Clybourne, the house where Destiny said she lived was dark. To him, it looked strange, almost abandoned. He got out of the car and took the letter she'd written to him from his pocket. He unfolded it and looked at it again. He was at the right place. What he didn't know was that Seneca and three other niggas were in the cut, waiting for him.

As Moo walked up to the porch, a dude walked from around the side of the crib. He looked to be about Moo's age so he asked him, "Yo, homie, Destiny here?"

"Yeah, she here," he said. "I'm her brother. Who is you?"

"I'm Moo, I'm supposed to pick her up for the dance," Moo replied with a smile.

"She's in there," he said. "You gotta go around the back and ring the bell, though." Then he brushed past Moo as if he was leaving.

When Moo got to the gangway, he saw three more grimy niggas lookin' in his direction. He tried to turn and leave but as he did so he met the muzzle of a .45 at his nose.

"Uh-uh, where you goin', nigga? Get your ass on back there." The nigga who claimed he was Destiny's brother had snuck up behind him.

Moo raised his hands. "What's going on?" he asked.

"This a robbery," the nigga said. "Don't make it no murder, nigga! Now shut the fuck up!"

Moo felt an arm wrap around his neck. He was being choked as he was dragged to the back of the house. He heard one of the niggas say, "Sen, I want that herringbone! Don't put no kinks in that bitch! When Moo heard Seneca's name, he realized that bitch Destiny had set him up.

Seneca slung him to the ground, pointing a 9mm at him Seneca said, "You lil' niggas never learn. Key look at this nigga! Take that shit off and hand it to my man. We want all yo' shit. You thought you was goin' to the dance with my bitch? You wanna dance, nigga?"

Moo took off his chain, his rings, and Rolex and handed them to Key.

"Stand yo' bitch-ass up!" Sen said, pulling him to his feet. Pointing his gun at Moo's feet, he said, "Dance nigga!" *Boom!* "You want my bitch?" *Boom! Boom! Boom!*

Boom! Boom! The gun sounded as Sen' let off shots at Moo's feet.

Moo danced around a few slugs, but one struck him in his left foot and he fell to the ground screaming in agony as the H.T.P. nig-gas stood over him laughing. Then Seneca hit him across his head with his pistol, knocking him out cold. When he regained con-sciousness, he was on his back facing the stars and bleeding from his head and foot. His pockets were pulled inside out and his lil' $1500 and Destiny's letter were gone. Although dizzy, he managed to make his way back to the car by hopping on one foot. He was relieved to see the keys still dangling from the ignition where he'd left them. He jumped into the car and stabbed out, making a vow right then to seek revenge and to never in life get played by another bitch. He drove himself to the hospital. Turned out the bullet went straight through his foot, hit the pavement, and bounced upward. They found fragments in his shoe. He was a minor, so of course, the hospital called Tip. She had a fit! Everyone rushed to the hospital because they'd only told Tip that Moo had been shot and didn't know where he had been hit. When the family got there, we were glad to see it was only his foot.

Chapter 9

A.T.K. Moo

Moo

When I returned to school I walked with a slight limp, but the foot seemed to be healing well. My A.T.K. niggas didn't even know what was going on. I hadn't seen them to tell them. Destiny played the game dirty. She'd put Seneca up on me from the jump. Of, course, niggas from 3 Chambers had a million and one questions. It was third hour and we were walking the hall.

"What up, nigga?" Phife asked, eager for information. "We know you hit that shit."

"Yeah, tell the truth. Did the pussy stank or was it good?" Jilla asked.

I said, "Jilla, yo' fool-ass loud as hell!"

"Ain't no coincidence both of y'all not showin' up at the dance," Tank said. "Yo' brotha been tryin' to feed us this *you sick* shit, but we know the real. She burnt you, huh?"

We all laughed.

"What hotel y'all go to?" Phife asked. "Who rented the room for y'all? You limpin' and shit. You put your leg in that pussy, huh? Can she fuck?" He was really laying the questions on me.

"Damn nigga, slow down," I said. "Maaan, y'all trippin'. A nigga caught the flu."

"Flu my ass, nigga. You on some secretive-ass shit, ain't you?" Tank asked, looking at me sideways.

"Nah, come on Doe, we gon' be late," I said. "I'll holla at y'all niggas at lunch, a'ight?"

As we branched off to go to our classes, Phife yelled. "Let me find out, nigga!" he said, smiling and shit.

I waved him off and kept moving. It was hard putting on a smile. Those niggas had run up into our spot as well as shot me. I was definitely feeling some kind of way about it.

Fourth hour came, Destiny's punk-ass couldn't even look at me. That shit egged niggas on even more.

"Look, she can't even look over here," Tank said. "Tore that pussy up! She been actin' funny all week. I wonder why?" They all laughed.

I wanted to go choke that hoe for what she'd done but, my plan was to wait it out and tell my niggas, then bring it to those niggas. Even at school, Doe and I were strapped nasty, so I was already in *wish a nigga would* mode. However, I was trying to chill until I put A.T.K. up on game. The last bell rang, and the day was over.

Me, Doe, Jilla, and the others walked out of the school's main entrance. I couldn't believe what I saw. Doe had told me he hadn't seen Seneca coming to pick Destiny up since I'd been absent. But this nigga had balls like Goliath! There he was, parked in front of the school, waiting.

"I see this nigga back," Phife said. "He ain't fuckin' her right. Is he, Moo?"

He was still talking but those were the last words I remember hearing. It's like I had tunnel vision. I blocked out all the chatter and movement around me. Scanning the hundreds of people out there, I saw Destiny making her way to the car. I can't explain it, but I just snapped! As I ran through the crowd I upped and started letting go!

Bak! Bak! Bak! Bak! Bak! Bak! Bak! Bak! Bak!

I shot dog's shit the fuck up and kept on running. I ran all the way home, fucked up foot and all. It wasn't long before the jakes had that bitch surrounded. They came in and got me. As I walked out of the house in cuffs, I saw Doe and everybody from Chambers standing out front. I just looked at them and nodded. Jilla, Tank, and Phife threw up the treys.

Doe yelled, "A.T.K., Moo!"

They put me in the wagon and pulled off. Once I got to the station, I found out I'd popped Seneca twice and hit Destiny three times. Neither one of them died, although they came close to it. I was originally charged with two attempted homicides, but my lawyer was hungry. So, he got my shit dropped to two counts of aggravated assault in possession of a deadly weapon. I ended up taking a plea for 4 ½ years in and 5 years out. They sent me to Ethan Allen Correctional Center for Boys. While I was down, of course, Teague and Doe kept in touch. The one thing I hated the most was that I'd started something that I wouldn't be there to finish. The war was on.

Doe, 3C, and nigga from the block were shooting it out with Hill Top on a daily basis. It shocked me when Doe told me he'd started reppin' 3 Chambers and rockin' with them niggas. He said A.T.K. was trying to squash some shit. He felt niggas were acting like bitches. Come to find out, the hype renting the spot was actually Key's auntie. He wanted to murk the bitch.

Doe said niggas from 3C were ridin' with him so I told him fuck Goldie 'nem, to just continue to collect our share of that money niggas was making and not to worry about anything else. None of the niggas from the block had come to see me. But Doe kept me laced with bread and plenty of flicks. Doe had finally enrolled in Rufus King. I couldn't wait to get home. The lil' chics Doe was sending me pictures of were stunning.

A year into my bid Phife was killed. It fucked me up, too. Word was it was those H.T.P. niggas. I hadn't realized how close Phife and I had become. I'd talked to him on the horn a few times and chopped shit with him raw the few times he and the squad came up with lil' bro. The same week he died bro and the others caught Seneca and Key with two bitches, coming out of the movie theater downtown and laid their asses down. Doe said the nigga, Key, had on all my jewelry, too. Haa! Nigga died with that shit.

The streets grew quiet after that. Bro and 3C opened up spots over on Center Street and Chambers. Bro was collecting on all ends. He gave a lawyer $50,000 on pop's behalf. The hood got salty because Doe spent all his time fuckin' with 3C and the lil' broads off the East. He hadn't told them he was through fuckin' with them. He wanted to keep that paper coming but niggas started acting funny with that. Doe said they had all kinds of new niggas off in the spot claiming A.T.K.

I told him to remain cool. I only had 22 months left. I told him when I got home I was collecting at least $30,000. They could give it up the easy way or I'd get it the Atkinson Teague way. Bro just laughed, but I wasn't bullshittin'.

Chapter 10

This Shit Ain't No Robbery, This Shit's a Given

Moo

Coming home after 3 ½ years was crazy. After being given credit for *good time,* I got out a few days shy of Doe's and my birthday. A lot had changed. Niggas had really come up. What fucked me up was seeing Hood and Shebba running around at 14 and 12 years old with ass and titties, niggas calling and coming by the crib! All that shit was going to stop! When I left Doe was drug-free. Now the nigga was smoking weed and shit. But it felt so good to be home. I went and got me some of that fie-ass pussy and some head from Lisa's thick ass. Plus, bro had a few buss downs for me. I fucked all day, no bullshit.

Tip cooked me some greens, cornbread, chicken, yams, and mac-n-cheese. I got it in and the hot sauce set it off! About 11:30 p.m. we were chillin' and Doe was telling me how he'd been seeing niggas from the hood here and there. How they got it up and how he hadn't been through there since our conversation about the collection agency I was starting. Yeah, niggas who owed pops had to pay their dues, too—with late fees. Fuck that, niggas eating meant niggas got dough. That's all I needed to hear.

"Grab me two bangers, Doe," I said.

"For what, nigga?" he asked, giving me that look.

"Cause we 'bout to go get what's ours, nigga. Them niggas been flippin' our money for years, it's time."

Doe handed me two .45s and asked, "First day home?"

"No half steppin'," I replied.

"A'ight, let's go." Doe grabbed two Glocks out of the closet, stuffed them inside his jeans, and headed for the bedroom door.

"Hold up, nigga," I said. "I know you got some drama attire around this bitch?"

"Aw, I got plenty."

"Well, put it on, nigga. These niggas gotta know we ain't fuckin' around." We put on black jogging pants and black hoodies.

***

11:48 p.m.

We hit Atkinson like we'd never left We walked up to the spot and hit the door with the code.

"Who dat?" a voice asked from behind the door.

"It's Moo, nigga!" Some nigga opened the door and just stared at us. "What the fuck you waitin' on? I know you know who the fuck we is. Open this muthafucka up!"

The nigga called for Goldie. "Yeah, what up?" The nigga must have been in the kitchen because we could hear him outside clear as day.

"The twins out here!" dog at the door yelled.

"Well, let 'em in then!"

Dude unlocked the screen door and stepped aside. I'd never seen the nigga before.

As we walked past him, Doe asked, "Who the fuck is you anyway?"

He ain't say shit. Big pussy had a shotty. Guess he was on security. We walked up the stairs and through the back door which led to the kitchen. A lot had changed, the spot was fully furnished as if a muthafucka actually lived there. The door to the back room was closed. Doe told me they had rented the upstairs, so the entire building was jumpin'. Goldie was sitting at the kitchen table with so much cash we could barely see him. A money counter was spitting out a wad of twenty-dollar bills he'd just loaded it with.

"Whatchu doin' out after 10 o'clock, nigga?" I asked.

He laughed as he stood up. "Ha-haa, Moo! What up, my nigga? Welcome home. When you get out?" He tried to hug a nigga, but I stopped him.

"Today," I replied.

"Damn, it's like that?"

"It is how you left a nigga," I said. "You niggas stopped hittin' bro off with that money. Left me high and dry upstate. Then y'all tried to squash unfinished business when it was on. Whatchu thought shit was all good? No letter, no nothin' but we should be good?"

"Doe, know it wasn't like that!" he said.

"Oh, how was it?" Doe asked.

"Man, I love y'all," Goldie said. "I'll pop my momma! Slap grams with the pistol! Y'all my niggas!"

"Save the theatrics, nigga," I said. "I tell you what—I want ten gees for every year I was gone. I did three and a half years so thirty-five will do, and that's bein' nice. What's these?" I grabbed a stack off the table.

"Thousand-dollar stacks," Goldie replied.

"Put thirty-five of 'em in the bag so we can get up outta here," I said.

He took a deep breath and blew it out. "Fuck it, a'ight," he said.

"Shit, since you love niggas so much, make that shit look like fifty," Doe said.

"Damn nigga!" Goldie said.

Click! Clack! We heard dude on *S* cock the shotty.

I upped on their asses so quick it was crazy. I had a .45 at Goldie's head and another one pointed at his big ass.

Doe laughed and said, "I don't think you wanna do that, big homie."

"Packman!" Goldie said. "What the fuck you doin'? Put the muthafuckin' gun down, nigga! This family."

"Yeah, Packman, put that shit down before I blow yo' shit back," I warned him. "This ain't no robbery. This shit's a given. Ain't that right, Goldie?"

Packman put the gun down. Goldie didn't say a word. He filled the bag up with our money and we got up out of there. But just as we were leaving Gina was riding through, breaking her neck, too. She saw us, and she recognized me because she had been one of the arresting officers when they came to get me after the shooting. She slowed down and stopped right in front of us. She rolled down the passenger side window. I handed the money to Doe and he got into the car.

"Moozeere, I see you out! You stayin' outta trouble?" she asked me.

I walked up to the car and leaned into it and said, "Yeah, I'm good. This you?"

"Boy, whatchu mean, is this me?" she asked.

"You a detective now, all undercover and shit?"

"Yup, homicide," she said. "You know that boy you shot got killed, don't you?"

"I was locked up, you can't put that on me," I said.

"Uh-huh. I know somebody who wasn't. What y'all got in the bag?"

"It ain't no body parts for sure," I said. "It's just some clothes I had to come grab real quick. Where Angie at?" I had to change the subject quickly to throw her off or at least try to do so.

"Why? Don't make me get out of this car! I'll bust a cap in your lil' ass and get away with it! I'm the police!"

"Yeah, yeah, I know," I said, smiling.

"And don't you forget it!" she said. "I got my eye on y'all. Don't be out here actin' no fool. I'd hate to be the one to come and get y'all."

"Again, huh?" I said.

"Yeah, again! Get away from my car with your crazy self. I gotta go."

"A'ight, Gina." I tapped her door and she pulled off.

Gina had been around forever. She used to come warn niggas when the *jump-out boys* would be coming through and who was about to get raided. Tuesdays and Thursdays were a bitch! If she hadn't been there when they came and got me a few years ago, I guarantee you they would have beat my ass and claimed I had been resisting or some shit.

I wondered if she knew about the spot. Probably not from the way the muthafucka looked from the outside. You'd never guess there were actually people in that bitch, and I hadn't seen her daughter, Angie since we switched schools. I wondered how she was doing. She was bad back then, I'm thinking she's got to be cold now.

I jumped into the whip with bruh and he asked, "What the fuck was that all about? What Gina say?" As he pulled from the curb, I knew he would ask questions.

"Shit, just bein' nosey as always," I replied. "But she did mention Seneca bitch-ass gettin' his shit peeled, though."

"What! What she say?" Doe asked, feeling uneasy.

"Relax, relaxxx, she just fishin'. You scary as hell," I laughed.

"I see you think shit's funny. Fuck you talkin' about! I ain't scared of shit!" Doe replied.

"Yo', I ain't know Gina was no mufuckin' homi' detec! What up with Angie? You been seein' her since my vacation upstate?"

"I-have I, maaan, Angie ain't the same Angie you remember no more."

"What chu mean?" I asked.

"I mean, Angie got dumb ass and some stupid-ass titties, nigga! Finer than a bitch! She runnin' around this mufucka callin' herself A.B."

"A.B., huh? Angie Burke, it makes sense."

"Hell yeah, but A.B. stands for *Any Bitch*. She proclaims to be the baddest. She says, 'go get any bitch.' She got shirts that say that shit and all. She be flexin' hard!"

"Damn, for real? She still be with the nigga, Boomer, all the time?"

"Yeah, they still runnin' around this bitch callin' each other brother and sister. I think they fuckin'. Shit, if the nigga ain't tryin' to fuck, he gay. As a matter of fact, I done seen the nigga Boomer with T-Dog, Goldie, and Ready on a few occasions."

"You bullshittin'! I thought he was a schoolboy. He ain't hoopin' no more?"

"Shittt, I don't even know. Don't let me get to lyin'."

"I don't really give a fuck one way or the other. If shit the way you say it is, I'm tryin' to see Angie!"

"She got thick as hell, I'm tellin' you. She go to Vincent. She ain't hard to find but just be careful, Cassanova. Remember the last one you chased cost you a bid."

"Yeah, I hear you. And best believe I'll never get caught slippin' again. What's with the bitch, Destiny, anyway? We couldn't inquire too much about her specifically over the wire bein' I got that no contact. But I do recall you tryin' to tell me somethin' in code last time we spoke."

"What I was tryin' to tell you was that after the shit went down at the theater, she moved to another state."

"She got the fuck outta Dodge, huh?"

"Yeah, she knew what was good for that ass. I couldn't get to her or she would've been dealt with."

"It's a'ight, she ain't get off scot-free. She caught a few hot ones. What's up with Teague? You hollered at 'em?" I asked.

"Yeah, I spoke to 'em about a week ago. He was supposed to had called today, but he didn't. You know the lawyers talkin' 'bout they need some more paper."

"What! I thought you just gave them fucks fifty more thou!"

"Shit, I did. Pops said they want some more."

"Well, how much you got stashed off the spots?"

"Don't even trip, I got a plan. I just gotta check with some of my peoples. I got a couple hundred thousand but I wanna make sure we stay straight. They'll suck us dry if we let 'em. You hear me?"

"What's the plan? Who yo' peoples and where the fuck we going? Tip crib ain't this way." I noticed we were heading Northbound.

"My peoples is them, two bitches, you had yo' lil' piece all up in earlier, nigga. And we ain't takin' this dough to Tip's just ride. I've been waitin' for the sun to go down so I could holla at you for real."

"Them lil' bitches off Chambers?" My face twisted in thought. "Yeah, Win and Yet, don't fall in love neither."

"What them lil' hoes gotta do with us gettin' money?" I asked.

"Just chill, I'll run it past you later on."

"What, nigga? Spit it out!"

"Look, just be cool. Let's go put this money up. Let me check on a few things then I'll holla at you, a'ight?"

"A'ight, I'm chillin', but you bet not be on no ill shit, nigga."

"Nah, you gon' love it, I promise. Remember, you was talkin' that collection agency shit? Well, we 'bout ta collect ugly. But first, I got somethin' I wanna show you."

Doe had bought a duplex out on Mill Road which nobody knew about. He had purchased the side-by-side specifically for my return to the streets. He wanted to show me that he'd stood on business while I was away.

"Who shit is that?" I asked. There was a white M.C., identical to the one we were in, parked further up the driveway.

"Just come on," Doe said, and we got out the car.

When we walked into the crib it was fully furnished. There was a big-screen TV, red oak floors and black Italian leather. The glass tables were trimmed in black and gold. I noticed a gold octagon in the living room held gold picture frames, but all of them were empty. I continued to look around.

"Yo', Doe, this shit is exquisite! Who the fuck lives here, bruh?" I asked, eyeing the Kenwood. The speakers, which sat in the different corners of the room, stood damn near as tall as I was.

"You like this joint?" Doe asked, throwin' the duffel bag on the sofa. "I see you done learned some new words in the joint. You think this is exquisite?"

"Hell yeah, nigga. This shit is tight!"

"Good, cause this you, nigga Welcome home." Doe threw me the keys.

"Huh? Ha-haaa, you bullshittin'!" I laughed, I couldn't believe it.

"Nope, this you. I live right next to you. This where we gon' lay our heads. Don't nobody know about these. Go ahead, check it out."

I went and checked out the kitchen and the three bedrooms. Then came back, grabbed my brother, and hugged him.

Doe said, "That's not all. That white M.C. outside, that's you, too. Plus, there's a safe built into the wall of the master bedroom closet with a hundred thou in it. The combo is our birthdays. The money we just took from Goldie is yours to do whatever you want as well."

"What the fuck? You runnin' 3C or some shit now, nigga?"

"Nah, bruh, we run it now. Go 'head and get settled in. I gotta run, go holla at my peeps, check a few spots. I 'll be back, though. We can rape the mall tomorrow. I gotta take
you to see my barber and get that raggedy-ass fade of yours shaped up. Ya shit can't be lookin' like that, rollin' with me."

"A'ight G.Q., you got that. I do need my shit cut. I think I wanna go Gumby or a Step." I rubbed my naps and said, "Go head and handle ya business. I'm chillin'." Then I flopped down on the love seat and reclined in the leather. I still couldn't believe everything Doe had just laid on me. Doe walked out the door smilin' with money on his mind.

Chapter 11

Hood

Moo's return home was a blessing in itself — we were all back together again. But, as the old saying goes, *"If it ain't one thing it's another."* Shebba had sickle cell anemia and it started acting up badly. Some days she was straight, but there were others when she couldn't make it out of bed. She could barely keep any food or liquids down, she threw up all the time. Her body would hurt so badly she'd cry herself to sleep. When she cried, I cried and that made all our asses cry.

I don't know what the fuck her doctors were on. How could her medication work one week and not the next week? It seemed we spent more time crying and praying than anything else. So, I asked Tip to take me to church. I felt God wasn't hearing our prayers from home and maybe he'd hear me there. Tip asked me over and over why I wanted to go to church on a Tuesday when she had to practically drag me there on Sundays. I didn't think she could answer my questions, so I never told her.

Well, she finally got fed up with my attitude and took me. She left Uncle Fry at the house to watch Shebba. When we got there we were welcomed by our pastor, Reverend Carpenter. I told him I wanted to talk to God. He looked at Tip then back at me. Tip shrugged her shoulders in a way that indicated she didn't know what the hell was going on. I walked past the pastor and got down on my knees right in front of the big stained-glass mural of Jesus crucifixion. I prayed for about an hour, unbothered. When I stood up, I was in tears.

"What's wrong?" the pastor asked.

"If God loves us so much. Why would He bring my sister into this world with sickle cell anemia? Why would He give her that disease?" I replied.

The pastor explained to me that disease doesn't come from God. I told him I'd read particular verses in the Bible where God inflicted sickness, and even death, upon His people. He told me that the Old

Testament laws no longer applied to us. He said it was the entire reason Jesus came to earth. He said God dealt with us differently back then because the world had become so sinful.

The people of that time actually thought it was okay to sin and commit murder because God didn't punish Cain for killing his brother. He actually protected him. He said God wanted to destroy the world but Moses asked Him to show mercy to us. So, God gave Moses laws to pass down to the people in order to make way for Jesus to come. No one was able to abide by the laws of the old covenant. We were in need of a Savior and Jesus' sacrifice cleansed us from all sin in the new covenant.

"Will Jesus take the pain away from my sister so we can live normal lives?" I asked the pastor.

"Keep praying," he told me.

But it seemed Shebba wasn't the only one I had to pray for, the streets said Moo and Doe were out there laying niggas down in the name of Teague. The streets were on fire. Moo hadn't been home a month and they were already on pure bullshit. Fifteen had lost their lives, 3C had lost two more. Dump and a nigga they called Gritty, even Goldie lost a few soldiers, although it wasn't a secret my brothers were originally from A.T.K. Bullets were flying in all directions. I was happy for the time being because God had answered my prayers.

Shebba was feeling better and was as vivacious as ever. However, we couldn't even stay at the crib. We were living in all sorts of different hotels until the beef was settled. The police were everywhere. The twins were relentlessly bodyin' shit. Niggas and their bitches got it if they were around when the dragons unleashed their fire. Also, nobody was getting any money because of the ongoing war. Therefore, Doe decided it was the perfect time to execute Plan B.

***

Yetta's Uncle Stan was the janitor at First Star National Bank on Wisconsin Avenue. He'd been working there for six years without a raise. So, he decided his boss's greed was blatantly and vicariously disrespectful. Subsidy was in order. Stan knew everything from the times' large amounts of cash would be dropped off by Brinks Security to what hours each employee worked, their lunch breaks, and who would most likely play hero if a threat to security arose. Doe and Moo had all the information they needed. They'd been casing the joint for months on end, parked outside the bank in a Mach 7 with tinted windows.

Wintress was behind the wheel, dressed in all-black. They were ready, Doe was armed with two Ninas and Moo cocked his Comper 15 while they listened to a police scanner. Even though it was only 12:15 p.m. in the afternoon, niggas who owed Teague were still feeling his wrath years later. As planned, a dope house on 29th in Wells had just been shot up. All available police units were responding, it was time.

"Win—four minutes! Don't move this muthafucka!" Doe instructed her through his mask.

"I got y'all, go!" she replied.

Moo and Doe got out of the car and ran into the bank, guns in hand. As soon as they entered the doors, Moo took control as he fired his weapon into the ceiling.

Blaka! Blaka! Blaka! Blaka! Blaka! Blaka!

A few screams could be heard from the bank's female personnel and clients. The men inside the bank were also shaken, hitting the deck, and hiding behind desks.

"Everybody get the fuck dowwnnn! Pops fucked up, right now!" Moo yelled as Doe rushed the tellers, jumping onto the counter. He had two duffel bags wrapped around his frame, with his guns extended he fanned his surroundings.

Then a fake-ass wannabe cop-security guard reached for his sidearm as he laid on the floor.

Boom! Yetta blew his brains out before he could even anticipate or load another thought. She had already been in the bank, wearing a trench coat, a curly wig, and sunglasses. They figured the ex-military vet wouldn't miss a chance to play victor — and they were right. Too bad the guy had paid little or no attention to the young lady lying on the floor next to him.

"Anybody else?" Moo asked menacingly, flourishing his weapon as Yetta jumped to her feet, brandishing two .38 Specials. She looked at Doe and nodded her head to the left at the man on the floor in a gray suit as she disarmed the dead security guard. She kicked the gun over to Moo.

"You!" Doe called out to the man on the floor in gray as he jumped off the counter.

Yetta took position over the tellers, making sure no alarms were set off.

"Get your ass up and come on!" he ordered. "We goin' to the vault!" He snatched the old man to his feet and walked the Larry King look-alike to the vault. "Three minutes!" Moo yelled, still waving his weapon.

Doe said, "You got ten seconds to open this bitch before I kill yo' ass!" He began his count, "One—two—" The vault was open by the time he reached the count of four. Doe couldn't believe his eyes. Money was just sitting there, wrapped in plastic, and stacked on pallets. "Here, fill these muthafuckas up!" he yelled, handing the old man the bags.

"Two minutes, thirty seconds!" Moo yelled.

The old man wasn't moving fast enough so Doe smacked him with one of the nines, knocking him unconscious. He filled the bags and threw them over his shoulders. They were so heavy he could barely walk.

"Cover me, we out!" Doe yelled, struggling with the bags.

Yetta kept her guns trained on the hostages lying on the floor as they backed out of the bank. Moo led them out with the assault rifle. The coast was clear, they jumped into the stolen Mach-7 and Wintress peeled off. The bank robbery was a success, they'd made off with 700,000 dollars and some change, and by the end of that summer, the beef had simmered. The twins bought the family all kinds of shit. They hit Stan and gave Teague's lawyers whatever they needed as well to continue his fight for freedom.

Shit, we were living so lavish that Tip decided to take in another family who had fallen on hard times. She was cool like that. She enjoyed helping people when she could.

Then Shebba became pregnant, I couldn't believe it. As many lil' niggas as the twins chased off, I was surprised anybody had the balls to risk getting fucked over. I mean, I called myself having a lil' boyfriend but the twins didn't know about him. Shebba had told me all about her little secret rendezvous with her lil' friend.

She said, "Ooh Hood, it hurt so good!" the first time she gave him a taste. Shit, I was nowhere near third base yet. A nigga could kiss me and suck the girls, but no goodies. Nope. So, it really scared me when she got pregnant. We kept it a secret for as long as we could which wasn't long. However, Tip didn't trip like we thought she would. But that didn't stop Moo and Doe from beating her baby daddy with bats.

Six months after our secret was revealed, Chauncy was born. However, our happiness was short-lived. Shebba's sickle cell started fucking with her again. I thought it was just another relapse that would soon pass. But this time we weren't so lucky. We lost her December 23rd of that year. It's crazy because it seemed as if though she knew. She would always say that she would die young.

The death of my sister changed everything in me and about me. I was mentally and emotionally drained and exhausted. I didn't understand how I could live with so much pain surging through me, I couldn't even focus. The New Year rolled in and we'd just buried my sister. Everybody was partying, popping champagne, and getting high. Me, I was sad, Tip told me Shebba was in a better place, trying to cheer me up. She told me that we should all make New Year's resolutions together in her memory. I told her I'd already made mine.

"Fuck the world, and I mean that!" I said as I stormed into my room and slammed the door. I didn't want to be bothered.

K'ajji

Chapter 12

Meec

Before Shebba died, I'd finally started attending Meec Junior High with her. But after all, that had happened during the Christmas holidays, going back there just wasn't the same. I was alone, everybody was whispering about her death. Shebba stayed into it with this bitch named Egypt because Shebba had stolen her so-called man. His name was Lasane Prince. He wasn't shit but he happened to be baby Chauncy's father. Egypt and her lil' crew must have thought it was real funny, fucking with me about our loss. They had no idea—I had a lot on my mind when they surrounded me on my way to lunch.

They were five deep, Egypt was right in front of me, Aletha was to my left, Nookie was to my right and Kaliah and Naomi were behind me.

"I see somebody ain't make it to school today," Egypt said, giggling as she switched her weight from one foot to the other, chewing hard on her gum.

I hated this pretty bitch! "Not now, bitch," I said. "I ain't in the mood." I tried to brush past her, but she stood directly in my path.

She said, "Awww y'all, Too Hood feelin' some kinda way cause her hoe-bitch sister died. Boo-hooo!" Then she rubbed her eyes, trying to clown me.

"Bitch, you gon' disrespect my sistah's memory!" I lunged, trying to put my hands on her, but Kaliah and Naomi grabbed me.

They shoved me to the floor and stood over me, mugging. I was so drained with grief, I didn't have the energy to bounce back to my feet.

As they walked off, I heard Egypt say, "That's what hoes get! Fuck her, I'm glad she's gone." They all laughed.

I got up and fixed my clothing, I didn't even go and eat. I went back to class. I sat in there in tears, thinking about Shebba. See, on the first day, I started attending Meec I had a few chicks trying to bully me. So, Shebba came to class with me on my second day of school.

She walked in and yelled, "Which one of y'all been messin' with my sistah? I'll beat all y'all asses!" The entire class just sat there in silence. The teacher didn't say shit. Shebba said, "Hood, meet me outside at the bus after school. If you got any problems, just point 'em out!" Then she walked out of the class. I hadn't had a problem since until today.

I opened my desk, grabbed a pair of scissors, and closed it. I stood up and put them in my pocket and walked out of the empty classroom. I was on my way to the chow hall. Those hoes had me fucked up. Ms. Carlton stopped me in the hallway, asking me where I was headed, sweating me about a pass. I lied and told her I had been in the bathroom because my stomach wasn't feeling too good however, it felt better and now I wanted to eat. She believed me and let me go.

I walked into the cafeteria and headed straight to the table where Egypt and her lil' crew sat every day. They saw me coming, too. I eased the scissors out of my pocket as I approached them. All of them remained seated except Egypt.

She jumped up and said, "Here comes this sick puppy. Come here doggy. Atta girl—arf—arf! Looks like you got somethin' there. What chu got?"

"I got this, bitch!" I shouted as I swung and stabbed her ass in the eye.

Egypt grabbed her eye and let out a loud shriek as blood and white shit gushed from her eye and her face. She looked down at her hand covered in blood and goop and took off running, holding her shit. Next, I went for Naomi and Kaliah's asses as they sat there looking stunned.

"Uh-huh! Yeeaaah, you hoes got jokes? Come on, I got a few myself—for all you bitches!" All of them jumped up and hit it. I chased them hoes all through the lunchroom until a teacher grabbed me.

All eyes were on me as Mr. Gordon screamed, "Ms. Phillups, drop the weapon!" He hugged me from behind, trying to stop me from chasing those hoes.

At the time, he was the only black teacher in the entire school. I had a lot of respect for him. So, I came out of my zone and dropped the scissors. He escorted me to the office. Well, you know the outcome, I was officially expelled from Meec. Later, I found out I had damaged Egypt's vitreous humor, her optic nerves, her iris, cornea, and the posterior chamber of her eye.

The police were called and I was charged. The bitch was blind in that one eye for damn near three years. I'd also sliced her face in the process. As a result, she'd not only be reminded of me every time she looked in the mirror but of Shebba as well. Her doctor bills were a bitch! Tip had to pay them and of course, she scolded me about all that happened. She told me I couldn't be trying to fight or kill everybody who said something I didn't like.

"But they disrespected Shebba's memory!" I protested.

She wasn't trying to hear me. Then Teague called. I heard Tip on the phone telling him, "Nall, I ain't whup her ass! I ain't got the energy for that shit no more, I'm tired!" I was sitting a few feet away from her, watching her boring-ass soap, General Hospital. She said, "Well, here she go. You wanna holla at her? Here, Hood." She handed me the phone.

I grabbed it. "Hello!" I yelled into the phone.

"What up, Too Hood?" he asked.

"Nothin', I'm chillin'."

"You chillin', huh? Well, why is you at school actin' a damn fool! That's not how pretty girls are supposed to act. Do you wanna end up in a place like this?"

"*Nope!*" I replied, putting extra emphasis on my *P*.

"Well, that's exactly where you headin' if you keep it up. Hear me?"

"But they—"

"But they nothin'! Look, promise me you gon' stop wildin' out and shit!"

"I don't know what that mean! They tried to treat me like I'ma bitch! I ain't no pussy—ass nigga!" I yelled.

"Girl, where is you getting' this shit from? You been hangin' around yo' damn brothas too much now! If I was out there, I'd tear yo' lil' ass up!" he yelled back.

"Teague, you ain't my daddy! You killed him, remember?" The phone went silent. I was dead wrong and I knew it. I knew I'd hurt him. He sighed. "Look, I'll see you when I get home," he said. "But we'll talk before that day comes. Put Tip back on the phone. I love you."

I didn't say shit, I just handed auntie the phone. I knew she was disappointed in me. She shot daggers at me, giving me a look that said, *"Bitch, I know you didn't."* Tip talked to Teague for the remaining time, while looking at me crazy the entire time.

Unified kept me out of school for damn near two months. Tip had to attend some type of school board meeting before they'd let me back in school. Then after all the smoke cleared, I was finally enrolled in Sara Scott — with Bri, Sweets, and Mula.

"P.Y.T. what up?" They greeted me with smiles on my first day of school.

Before I knew it, it was our 8th-grade year. We were growing up, stuffing our bras, and getting into boys. Our popularity went through the roof when we joined the basketball team. It was there that we made our pact. The following year our next move would be to Riverside High and we'd never separate again.

Chapter 13

Sonny's

Thursdays were ladies' nights at Sonny's. Surrounded by women, Moo, Doe, O'Jilla and some more of 3C sat in booths, sipping Hen, and popping champagne in the V.l.P. section of Sonny's on Broadway. Atkinson Goldie, Ready, T-Dog, Prince, and their crew sat directly across the room. Both squads were showing out, throwing money, and trying their hardest to clown each other. Goldie's money was long, but after seeing the stacks of hundreds Doe had just thrown into the air, he wasn't too sure he was holding more than the twins. A.B. was in the building but Boomer was all over her.

They were on the dance floor, grinding to *Living for the Love of You* by *Al Green*. Moo found himself jocking her style. Although a handful of chicks were at him that night, he wanted Angie. He wasn't even paying much attention to the lady right in front of him, and she was sitting on his lap. His eyes were stuck on A.B. He was imagining what he would and could do if he had the opportunity to get ahold of her. She moved her body seductively, knowing she was the baddest bitch in the establishment.

Deejay Michael Hightower had just spun *As We Lay* by *Shirley Murdock* when John LeVon walked in. He and his posse rolled in about twenty deep. On the other hand, 3C was more than fifty strong throughout the club, all of them strapped nasty. Yelling over the music, Jilla got Moo's attention, pointing out the O.G.'s arrival.

"Twin, yo', check it! Ain't that dog y'all been tryin' see 'bout them scratches right there?" Jilla nodded toward the entourage.

"Watch out. Who that be?" Moo asked, pushing the skimpily clad Darneesha off his lap. She was a broad he'd just met that night.

Doe also took notice, he said, "Yeah, that's the nigga John LeVon over there that used to kick it with pops 'nem back in the day. You remember Slim, don't you?" Doe smiled.

"Oh, yeeahh. How could I forget?" Moo said. "The nigga finally decides to show his head, huh? We 'bout ta go holla at 'em." Moo adjusted his burner.

"For what? We got money to burn and the lawyers done already been taken care of," Doe replied, still chillin' with his lil' honey out of Illinois. He'd been seeing Jahnahdah for years now.

"One can never have too much capital," Moo said. "Besides, the nigga owes us! Fuck we look like lettin' this hoe-nigga walk around like he ain't bite the hand that fed 'em. Teague said he was holdin' over two-hundred bricks of that raw when them people kidnapped him for ransom, right?"

"Right." Doe rubbed his chin, looking over at the old heads.

"Anyway, fuck all that shit! Is you comin' or what, nigga?" Moo was feeling impatient.

"Yeah, of course, I'm comin'. Hold up a see! Let me holla at baby real quick. Damn nigga, is we just hollin' or we 'bout to get on some murder shit?" Doe asked, still smilin'.

"Shit, I don't know how this shit gon' play out. So, tell ya, girl, they need to be headin' towards the nearest exit cause if anybody moves, everybody dyin'," Moo replied.

Jahnahdah hated Moo's devious ways. She wanted to cuss his ass out. He always knew how to fuck up a perfectly good night. She, Mona, and the rest of her crew got up and casually walked out of the V.I.P. section towards the exit, careful not to cause a scene.

The twins had grown into young men since the last time John had seen them. They looked like Teague times two. He and his men were at the bar ordering drinks. Sending thirty or so 3C hard hitters ahead of them, Moo and Doe played the background as they approached J. L. and all who stood with him. Soon, John and his team of gangstas were surrounded. One of his men took notice and quickly got his attention. He tapped him on his shoulder as John whispered into the ear of something fine that was seated next to him.

"J. L., I think we got a problem," Burleigh Rick said, looking on as the 3C members closed in. He was J. L.'s cousin and right-hand man.

"What—what chu—" J. L. said as he turned around.

The sinister and deadly looks on their faces along with how they clutched their weapons said they meant business. The Kangos, Adidas, and Puma attire with the dookie ropes and gold nuggets said

The Streets Will Never Close

they were young. He was wondering what could've been the problem? He and Sonny went way back. Then, in the shadows, he thought he'd seen a ghost from his past, someone he thought he'd never see again in this lifetime. There he was again in different clothing. But how? The two binary stars stepped forward, resembling their father. Then it clicked in his mind exactly who they were.

"What up old head?" Moo accosted him. "You remember Atkinson Teague, don't you, nigga?"

J. L. tried to laugh it off. "Yeah—yea—yeah! Twins—ha-haaa! I remember y'all! How y'all—"

Doe shut that shit down immediately. "Nah, this ain't dat, nigga! This ain't no fuckin' happy family reunion! You best be rememberin' my pops left you out here with a whole lotta product in these streets! It's time you pay yo' dues. Hear me? Now we seen y'all march up in this bitch. Gotcha minks on with your gold and shit. That's real nice, but the Superfly era is over, nigga! We gotta have everything you owe, with interest!"

"Hold up now. Y'all comin' at me all—" he tried to say with this smirk on his face.

"You heard what the fuck my brotha just said, nigga!" Moo said. "And you smilin' and shit! Do it look like we fuckin' playin'?"

Doe laughed, looking around. John LeVon's men were smart enough to know not to move. They were outnumbered as well as outgunned. J. L. no longer wore a smile. Shit had just gotten real.

"Damn, now see, I don't think you should say another word," Doe said. "Listen, let's be reasonable. You know pops been down a minute and you ain't wrote, sent no bread, no nothin', right? I mean, that's a rhetorical question there. We all know the answer to that, or you wouldn't be standin' here with all these guns pointed at you. So, this what it is. We want three mil and four hundred bricks by next weekend. We'll be in touch to let you know where we want it delivered. Now, with that said, I'd advise y'all to get the fuck up outta here before my niggas get to flashin' and you and yours get to dyin' in this bitch."

J. L. and his camp wisely took his advice and headed towards the exit.

Moo yelled, "And don't start duckin' us either, nigga!"

J. L. turned and looked back, but kept it movin'.

"The look in that nigga's eyes say we gon' have to kill his ass," Doe said. "We should've flashed on his ass right here."

"I'm knowin'," Moo replied. "But there's too many eyes watchin' us." Indeed, there were.

Chapter 14

Goldie

Last week, me and mine sat back and watched as that shit went down between the twins and John LeVon. Everybody from 3C upped their guns. Of course, Prince, T-Dog, and Ready wanted to move when they saw the shit getting ugly, but I told them to fall back.

I told them, *"It's more than enough guns pointed at them, niggas! They got it!"* I said, stepping in front of them.

By the look of things, it seemed it was unimaginable that any of J. L.'s people would have survived if 3C got to dumping in that bitch. Even bitches from over that way showed they weren't gun-shy. I know what you've got to be thinking, *Why the hell would my niggas want to help Moo and Doe after they came at me sideways?* Well, I didn't exactly tell them the entire truth. I mentioned that they came through and I gave them $50,000, but that's it. Packman is the only one who knew everything, and I made sure he kept his mutha-fuckin' mouth shut!

I got my own plans for them niggas. The shit that went down at Sonny's played right into it, the enemy of my enemy is my friend. You'd never guess who's seated a few seats ahead of me, flying first class to Jamaica. John and his wife, Cuppy. They're accompanied by two of his henchmen. Now, all I got to do is find the right time to holla at them.

***

J. L.

I made my way down to the beach where Cuppy was waiting on me. I'd just gotten off the phone with Burleigh Rick. Everything was a go, our plan was in motion. These young niggas had no idea who they were fucking with. If they thought, they were going to extort me like I'm a bitch, they had another thing coming. I don't know what kind of asylum they got Teague locked up in that he thought sending his kids at me was going to move something. Yeah, clearly I'm bogus for not looking out for him when those people got ahold of him.

That's not how real niggas rock. Teague fucked with me the long way, too. He looked out for me when nobody else would and I betrayed him. There's no excuse for my greed. I was actually scared shitless when those indictments rolled in. The Feds weren't bull-shitting, they were tracking niggas down and putting those football numbers to their asses. They hit our spots over on 10th in Atkinson, the spots on 24th in Brown, the spots on 16th in North, and the spots on 26th in Center.

Teague caught the most charges by far. I hid for months, knowing I was on that list of the wanted. Surprisingly, they missed me and that left the streets wide open for the taking, so I took them. I started fucking with my cousin, Rick, because all our players were hot, or had already been indicted. I needed niggas to move the product so I sewed up Burleigh first then everything around me. I brought quite a few killers onto the team but Po Kelly was the most lethal. He, Rick, and L. Ross were about to make the drop to the twins.

Fuck them! It's what they asked for. I was laid up with my boo-thang on the white sands off the shore outside our villa in Jamaica, sipping a Daiquiri made with that special rum they got over here, when some nigga approached us. My security detail upped on his ass.

The nigga saw those thangs and put his hands up screaming, "I come in peace!" He said his name was Atkinson Goldie. It's a name I'd heard before from back home.

"Hold up—don't—don't shoot god damnit! It's me, I'm the one that sent your people that information."

Chapter 15

Doe

11:02 a.m.

Me, Moo, Jilla, Tank, Smoke as well as block niggas, to those who moved bricks and a bunch of the 3C niggas were all at the spot on Chambers trying to come up with some answers. Three days ago, two of our lil' niggas went missing. Smoke said the last time he saw them they were leaving the spot over on Center Street. Apparently, he was the last one to lay eyes on them in the hood, that we knew of.

Too Deep and Joshie were fifteen and sixteen with Joshie being the oldest. They were young but their loyalty to the team was unquestionable. A few niggas had their own ideas. Some cogitated and actually believed they'd run off with what little dope and money they had in their possession. But why would they do that? I knew off the top that wasn't the case. They'd made more and handed over 50 times that amount. The main two suggesting my niggas had pulled a dope-fiend move were brothers, Six and Crook.

Crook didn't like Joshie because Lil' Joshie had beat that ass on several occasions. Six was just riding with his older brother which was understandable. So, I took the floor, I'd heard enough of this bullshit. Period!

"A'ight everybody, listen the fuck up! Ain't no muthafuckin' way they ran off with shit! Y'all can freeze that shit, right now! This what we gon' do! Smoke, you, Thirty-eight, and Brew gather the rest of the lil' niggas! I'm shuttin' shit down! I want y'all to keep searchin'! Low end to the Zoo. If we done hit it already, hit it again!

"All of Chambers, Aure, Hopkins, Burleigh, Garfield, and all the way through Fondulac! Hit malls, arcades, barbershops. etcetera! In the meantime, we 'bout to head out by their mommas, their sisters, and their aunties' cribs! Find us somebody out there that can tell us somethin'! Everybody meet us back here by four p.m., worse case, is don't nobody find 'em. If y'all hear anything or see 'em, hit us on the hip!

"Keep y'all guns at hand in enemy territories! Their people done already reported 'em as missin', so be careful. The police out there lookin' for them lil' niggas, too. Now, get y'all asses outta here! Put two in behind the pages if y'all run into Too Deep! And put five in if y'all come across Joshie! Most likely they together!" I yelled behind them.

Across town on 19th and Burleigh, Too Deep and Joshie were in the basement of one of J.L.'s old dope houses. He'd shut it down and pushed clientele to another location for purposes such as this. Duct-taped to chairs, they were at the mercy of three of Milwaukee's known killers and their primitive savagery. Leonard Ross, Po Kelly, and Burleigh Rick had taken turns going in on the young 3C members. Three days in the same position with no food or water, they were already damn near dead.

However, death wouldn't come that easy. Their eyelids had been sliced from their faces, their knees were crushed with a sledgehammer, all their fingers had been cut off and seared with a blowtorch, leaving only their thumbs. But sadly, their pain had just begun. As he came back down the stairs, the buzzing sound of a chainsaw and the demon-possessed look on Po Kelly's face had them terrified.

Po sang, "Ready or not here I come lil' niggazzz!"

***

Meanwhile, Ross and Burleigh Rick were upstairs sitting at the kitchen table, eating breakfast.

"Shit, I thought I was crazy. That nigga Po got me, though." Burleigh Rick took a bite of his crisp bacon.

"Geh me my money, nigga! Ha! I told you I saw somethin' in those lil niggaz. I told yo' ass they wouldn't break. Now, geh me my cash, and don't get no syrup on it either!" Ross held out his hand.

"Yeah, yeah, fuck you!" Burleigh Rick slid back from the table. His humongous size made it difficult for him to reach into his pocket while seated. The struggle was real, and beads of sweat formed across his forehead as he struggled to get his hand in his pocket.

"You ain't gonna make it, nigga. Stand your big ass up." Ross was laughing.

Burleigh Rick didn't find shit funny. He was frustrated over being wrong and losing the bet. He stood up, went into his pocket, and pulled out a stack of money. While counting out two thousand dollars to pay Ross, they heard their latest victim's screams coming through the walls and floorboards.

Below them, Po was putting in work.

Kʼajji

Chapter 16

Moo

45 Minutes Later

Doe and I were the last two heading out of the spot. I knew we had to be feeling the same thing, he just didn't know how to say it. So, I asked him.

"What up? You think the nigga, John LeVon got the lil' homies?"

"It's a possibility that I'm not ready to face, right now," Doe said. "I'm knowin' he could be behind it. But, damn, I guess I'm just hopin' for the best, right now."

"You ain't forgot that today is the day he's supposed to drop that money and them demos off, have you?" I asked.

"Nah, it's scheduled for tonight at 7:00 p.m. at the spot on Ring. Jilla and Tank gon' handle the drop. Why, what up?"

"I don't know, I just got this feelin', you know? In the joint, an old head told me somethin' that has stuck with me ever since he said it."

"What he say?" Doe asked.

"He said, 'I survived cause I'm worth survivin'. Winning ain't everything, it's the only thing. Therefore, for every action, there's a reaction.' Doe, as you know, the game is changin'. He old school but there's somethin' tellin' me that he's different than the one's we've dealt with in the past. We gotta be careful. His money long so we wanna be wise and out think this nigga."

"So, whatchu sayin'? You think he had somethin' to do with Too Deep and Joshie comin' up missin'?"

"I'm damn near positive. Come on, though. Let's ride down and check on they people just to make sure. I could be wrong."

As we rode North towards 82nd in Medford to Joshie's momma's crib, bro got a page, it was Tank. My shit started blowin' up as well.

K'ajji

***

Doe

Me and Moo sped down Burleigh and hit Fondulac on a mission. For all of you who don't know the Mil, Fondulac will take you straight through the city. We rode with caution, watching for any kind of signs of my lil' folks — the rollers and bitch niggas. We'd damn near made it to my lil' nigga's momma's crib when my hitter went off. Moo shit went off right after mine. I was geeked!

"What, who the fuck?" Moo questioned, looking at his pager as he drove.

"Yo, shit say, 8-2-5-6—2-5 2-5 1041-911?" I asked with a big smile on my face.

"Hell yeah! What yours say?"

"It says you wrong, nigga! They found the lil' homies! That's Tank, they over at the spot-on Ring! Buss a yewy, nigga! Hurry up! Them lil' niggas better have a good excuse or I'm about to beat they lil' asses!" I laughed.

So, we turned around and headed back top speed, to Fondulac, to The Zoo. But when we finally hit 10th and Burleigh, a police car was parked in the middle of the street. It was posted at an angle in the middle of the block so we couldn't buss a left to get to the spot. We could see the entire neighborhood was standing outside on the corners, *look-a-whoin'*. We ended up parking on 9th and walking down there to see what was going on. The first thing on my mind was we had gotten hit and the police were around there bringing niggas out in cuffs, typical hood shit.

Word must have gotten out that we'd just pulled up and was on our way around there. Trina, Chanel, Ava, and Taliah approached us in tears. This was A.B.'s lil' crew but she wasn't with them. Their eyes and the look on their faces said a million words, but I was still in denial.

"Moo-Moo and Doe-Doe don't—don't do it. Don't go around there. It's too muuccchhh! An—and it's to—too many policemen around there," Liah said, barely able to speak.

80

I looked past them and saw some of our lil' niggas coming our way. I threw up my hands. "What up? What the fuck happened? The spot get hit or somethin'? Where them lil' niggaz at?"

Thirty, Smoke and Freaky stood before us, shaking their heads in anger. Then Thirty said, "I wish shit was that simple, big homie. At least then we'd be able to go see 'em."

I was still lost. Shit, Thirty was only thirteen. We called him Thirty-eight because the lil' nigga acted and said shit beyond his years.

Smoke said, "Tank came over this way to shut shit down. But when he pulled up, he saw two barrels sittin' on the sidewalk in front of the crib. One of 'em had a note taped to it that said, *THE PACKAGE*. The barrels had blood seepin' from the bottom of 'em. Then he opened the first one, he saw Too Deep up in that bitch chopped up. They dead, dog." Smoke dropped his head.

"Get the fuck outta here! You bullshittin'! Ain't no mufuckin' barrels, nigga!" I pushed through everybody standing in front of me. I walked to the corner of 10th in Ring. The black and yellow tape indicated I couldn't go any further. Fuck that!

I tried to cross the barrier, but a policeman grabbed me. "Wait! Waaaiiittt, sir! You can't—you can't go down there!" He grabbed me as soon as I ducked under that shit.

Looking over his shoulder as we tussled, I saw them. I saw the barrels, it was true. The pain hit me in my head and my chest.

"Don't fight me on this, or I'll have to arrest you! What's your name, son? Those your friends down there?" He grasped my shoulders, trying to look me in my eyes.

"Get the fuck off me!" I pushed him up off me. But the single tear which ran down my face and the mug I gave him surely answered his question. I ducked back under that shit and walked off mugging as the entire neighborhood watched and whispered.

When I got back to my niggas I asked, "Where everybody else at?"

Freaky said, "They arrested Block, Tank, and Jilla on some disorderly conduct shit. The police were tryin' to stand on some shit, talkin' about goin' up in the spot lookin' for suspects.

You already know, Tank snapped. Block and Jilla just followed suit. Everything's good, though. Bella and Telesis left with the work and everything before they even got there. They around the corner at Bell momma tip."

"Well, y'all know what time it is," I said. "Load up, call everybody! Tell 'em the twins said to meet us on 3C. Body count!"

Chapter 17

MPD Detective Gina Burke

I arrived on the scene about an hour ago. "Damn, what y'all lookin' at! Take y'all asses in the house!" These people were nosey as hell when they didn't need to be. "Anybody see who dropped these barrels off?" I yelled to all the spectators standing around staring at me. "I see ain't nobody got no damn job! DeMeo, you see who dropped these barrels off?"

"No," he replied, shaking his head.

He was probably lying. "How about you, Ms. Russel? I know you saw something?"

"Nope!" she replied, rolling her eyes.

I couldn't believe she was damn near eighty and acting like she was eighteen. "It's a Sunday in September! Its sixty-three degrees in the middle of the afternoon! It's what—a hundred and twenty of y'all out here! And ain't nobody see who dropped these big-ass— hmph! Y'all know what? No names! I just need the color of the truck! A van! A license plate number! *Anything!*" I looked at the crowd. "Silence, huh? Y'all know—y'all know them, babies, in there, right? Yup, they cut 'em down! Like—like their lives didn't even matter! Like they were cows or pigs or some shit! Ms. Freemon! How old is your daughter, Ronnie?" I asked, already knowing the answer.

"Sixteen!" she replied.

"Sixteen! Y'all hear that? Sixteen! I know she knew these boys! Crook, I see you! Didn't you know Too Deep and Lil' Joshie?"

He dropped his head. "Yeah, I know 'em."

"Six, what about you? Nothin', huh? I know y'all done seen these babies around here! They lived right around the corner! Some of y'all kids ran with 'em! They were fifteen and sixteen! Y'all ain't see nothin'?"

***

I was done with my investigation. The crime scene investigation unit was loading the barrels into their van to be transferred downtown. We would need to remove the bodies very carefully to preserve any evidence undetectable to the human eye that only technology could pick up. But I had one more thing to say to this community of people, *my people*. They all resembled me in some form or another.

"This could very well be you! Your child! Your friend! Your brother, nephew, daughter, sister, or cousin! Whatever they've done, they didn't deserve this! I know they sold dope, carried pistols, and some more shit! Their names came through the station countless times, mentioned in all kinds of shit! But Joshie Evers and Tomorrow De'pere were just young boys that made mistakes! The greatest tragedy in this life is not death. It's living life without purpose! That's why I chose to make a difference. This shit has got to stop! Now, when I leave here if anybody wants to come forward, y'all know where to find me!"

Just as I finished saying what I had to say, a blue Buick LeSabre came to a screeching halt at the corner of 10th in Ring, gaining all our attention. A woman jumped out of the passenger side of the car.

"Joshieeee!" she wailed, running through the police tape. Officer Newman grabbed her and hugged her. "My—my son down theeerrreee! Let me goooo, Joshieee!" she cried, trying to get away from the officer.

Walking towards her I yelled, "Let her through!" *Damn Joanne*, I thought as she ran straight into my arms. She was a mother just like me.

Chapter 18

Heat

The temperature dropped significantly as the sun set into night's dusk, bringing what some thought was the ending to one of that summer's bloodiest days. The block was packed.

However, the cessation of life was just beginning. Wearing a Yosemite Sam mask under his hoodie, Doe clutched his weapons. Moo was also blacked out and right by his side. A Marvin the Martian mask concealed his identity. They were crouched down beside a house in the middle of 34th and Burleigh. This area was what niggas referred to as Zoo territory.

It was also a block J.L. controlled and moved heavy product. Niggas and bitches alike were out on the block, kicking it as if hours earlier their head honcho hadn't sent their lil' homies back to them—minced and mutilated—as a clear sign of war. Their lack of concern of retaliation only added fuel to the fire which burned inside of them. Moo and Doe rose up and came out the cut, flockin' shit down. Those who weren't immediately hit, scattered in different directions as Moo let the Kalashnikov ride. Doe banged out two .357s.

Boom! Boom! Boom! Boom! Flocka! Flaka! Flaka! Flaka! Flaka! Flaka! Flaka! Flaka! Flaka! Boom! Boom! Flaka! Flaka! Flaka!

There would be no escape without injury or certain death. Wintress, Yetta, Smoke, and Freaky took positions at the end of the block, laying shit down! Masked as Babs, Lola, Sylvester, and Bugs, they let go!

Tat! Tat! Tat! Blat! Tat! Tat! Tat! Bak! Bak! Bak! Bak! Bak! Lah! Lah! Lah! Lah! Duc! Duc! Duc! Duc! Duc!

Lil' Zoo and Famo tried to shoot back but they were outgunned. Caught off guard and under the influence of liquor and weed, they were slow and sloppy. Blue reached and was laid down right away. As the smoke cleared, the 3C members had disappeared into the night. Screams could be heard from blocks away. The morning newscast dubbed those responsible for the methodical onslaught as, *The Loonies*.

Eleven people lost their lives and seven were severely injured. Sheena, Jamie, Shay, and Rena were the only survivors of all the females out there. Five of their home-girls had lost their lives. When J. L. got the call in Jamaica, needless to say, he was livid.

Chapter 19

Hood

I'll never forget it, it was my freshman year in high school, a Monday morning. My brothers came into my room and woke me up. It was three in the morning.

"Hood, Hood, getcha ass up!" Moo whispered, nudging me.

I rolled over. "What the hell?" I said groggily.

They were both dressed in all black, I sat up.

"Here, take these." He was holding two chrome .45s. He handed them to me. Both of them had this look in their eyes, a look I'd never seen before.

"Twins, what's wrong?" I asked them. "What's goin' on?" I held the two guns in my hands, wrenching worry etched across my face.

"Nothin'," Moo said. "Look, you know we been warrin' with these niggaz. You can't be layin' up in here all comfortable, sleepin', and shit. Get up, we need you to sleep out on the couch by the front door. Uncle Fry got the back. We tried to move y'all until this shit is over with.

"But Tip ain't leavin'," Doe said. "You remember everything we showed you?"

"Yeah, point and shoot, never hesitate. But what about school?" I asked.

"You stayin' home for a couple of days," Moo said. "Here— here go some extra clips. How many shots you got?" He was testing me.

"They full?" I asked, checking the chambers and droppin' the clips. "I got fourteen, one on top, six in the clips, and twelve once I reload."

"Tip got an automatic shotgun," Moo said. "Fry holdin' all kinds of shit. Tip ain't gon' come out of her room unless it's to use the bathroom. You gotta cook and make sure she good on her Pepsi and shit. We got some niggaz posted outside, so don't worry. This is just a safety precaution."

"Whyyy? Why they gon' be out there? Where y'all goin?" I asked.

"We gotta handle some business," Doe said. "We'll be back soon, though. Y'all need anything, Jilla gon' be right out front. Now come on."

As I walked out of my room, I saw Unk posted by the back door with a Mac .90. He just nodded as if though there was nothing unusual about his niece comin' out her room in her PJ's carryin' two .45s. There was, indeed, a duffel bag filled with guns at his side. Tip had her door shut. Moo and Doe were on my heels. They walked me to the living room to the couch, threw my pillow, and covers on the sofa then both hugged me at the same time.

As I looked at them, Moo said, "Anything come through this door kill it."

"On Shunbria, I got this!" I said. "But y'all better bring y'all asses back!" Tears started flowing out of nowhere.

"Don't cry, sis. We comin' back," Doe said, opening the front door.

Moo smiled and said, "Hell or high water. Lock this door behind us. See you in a few." He kissed me on my cheek, and they left.

***

Doe

We crept silently out of the crib into the a.m. Word had gotten back to us that J.L. and those Burleigh niggas were supposed to be coming at us full throttle and hitting the crib. Moo and I had no idea whether they knew about the spots out on Mill Road, or whether they were talking about Tip's crib. To be safe, we moved all our cash to a third location out on 95th in Fondulac which we'd just copped for the fuck of it. It was funny how the streets talked, while the nigga we were really after was resting on some exotic island, his folks were here suffering. I got to give it to him, though, that's boss shit when a nigga can send shots from a distance.

However, the only problem with that was when you're away it's hard to protect your family. We decided if we couldn't get ahold of him, we'd grab and take something close to him. His nephew, Lil' Zoo, was one of many who'd got hit when we flashed on niggas this morning. We'd been watching family members of the surviving victims come and go. The hospital was packed with the police or we would have run up into that joint and put an end to their asses like we intended. They didn't deserve to live, my lil' niggas wasn't breathing.

We recognized Zoo's momma from the news coverage and decided to follow her ass home out there in Jade Garden. Just in case, we had to get on some grimy shit. A flip of the coin and that's exactly what we were on. There are no rules in war. Shit, anybody can get it.

***

Moo

It was 4:50 a.m. and we were sitting in her kitchen eating sandwiches, munching on some Ruffles, and sipping on some Kool-Aid. Then she walked in, wearing just her panties and bra, surprised to see us.

"Damn!" I said.

"Mmm, good morning!" Doe said.

Zoo's momma was stacked, strapped, big-busted and fine coming out of her sleep! She screamed and tried to run, but Doe caught her and snatched her ass up.

"Bring yo' ass here! Where you goin'?"

"No! No! Noo! What y'all dooiinnn'?" she screamed.

"Bitch shut the fuck up!" Doe said and smacked her with the banger.

She was still conscious, but barely. We dragged her ass into the garage of her condo. After we gagged, roped, and tied her ass up, we went back inside and finished our snacks. Then we washed the dishes we'd used and wiped everything down. We left no trace of us ever having been there. She was coming with us this morning.

Chapter 20

Hood

Bri, Karm, and Mula came by to see why I'd been absent from school. They knocked on the back door and as soon as Fry opened it, they marched in.

"She in 'nere, gon' yonder!" he said with his country ass.

Then all I heard was Mula, "P.Y.T., Hood, all them niggas posted around the house! Nah, uh-uh."

I heard them open my bedroom door only to see I wasn't there. Then I heard Bri, they were getting warmer.

"Where she at? Hood, niggaz is in all—" She stopped talking as they entered the living room and I was standing there pointing my two old ladies at them.

"Freeze hoes!" I said with a smile. They paused then all of them rushed me.

"Ooh, bitch where you get them from?" Bri whispered. They were all as fascinated as I was.

"Moo and Doe gave them to me," I replied. "Y'all know I hold shit down." I was jacking hard.

I told them what Moo and Doe told me about the beef. Shit, they grabbed a couple of units out the bag Uncle Fry had, and we all sat around scared, but ready for whatever. I had already taught them everything I knew about the artillery, so they knew how to handle shit. We called Lue but her momma wouldn't let her out the house after hearing about all the females that had just gotten killed while fucking around in The Zoo.

The day went by fine but that night was an entirely different story. It was around 7:15 p.m. I was worried because I hadn't heard from my brothers in over ten hours. I thought their asses would have at least called. Ignoring Jilla's warnings to stay away from the windows, I walked over to peek through the curtain. It seemed as soon as I touched the curtain, multiple gunshots rang out in front of the crib.

Lah! Lah! Lah! Lah! Boom! Boom! Boom! Boom! Loc! Loc! Loc! Loc! Loc! Doom! Doom!
We dove to the floor, rolling over onto our backs. We all had our guns trained on the front door. Shots were still being fired.

"Shit, Hood! I'm scarrreddd!" Karm said.

"Stay calm, Sweets," I called Karm by her nickname. "We gon' be a'ight! You ain't ready to die, is you?"

"Hell nall, bitch!" she replied, hands shaking violently as she held her aim.

"Well, don't die then," I said. "You feel that Sweets?"

"Feel what?" she asked.

"That big-ass shotty in between your legs! You chose it! It didn't choose you. It holds the power of life and death," I said. *Clack! Clack!* She jacked the slide. "Yeeaahhh, bitch! That's what I'm talkin' 'bout! Mula, Bri, y'all good?" I glanced to my right and then to my left.

"I'm good!" Mula replied, holding her own steady, ready to bang out two nines.

"Let these bitches come!" Bri said. "Let 'em come, Hood!" I thought I heard some cracking in her voice.

"Bri, you cryin'?" I asked, knowing I was just as spooked as she was.

"A few tears—just a few," she replied. "But it ain't nothin' I can't handle. I'm good, bitch!"

I noticed the gunfire had ceased and there was this dreadful silence in the room. As we waited, guns in our hands, it was like death coming but we just couldn't hear it. Then all of a sudden we heard giggling coming from behind us. Looking above our heads, it was the twins!

"Dayum, I see y'all about that action," Doe said, smiling.

Moo said, "So serious." He had his arms crossed, smiling, and chewing on a damn toothpick.

I threw my guns on the loveseat. "Boy!" I said, punching the closest one to me which happened to be Doe. "Where the hell y'all been? And what the fuck y'all got goin' on out there?" Doe was laughing and shit. I didn't see a damn thing funny.

"Two carloads full of Zoo niggaz came through dumpin'," Moo said. "We flashed on they ass, though. You can relax. A few of 'em gone permanently. They crashed into a parked car around the comer."

"Yeah," Doe said. "Let's just say it was their last ride."

"How the hell they know where we live anywayz?" I asked, walking up to Moo to punch his ass next. He said, "Girl, watch out!" He pushed me to the side. "That's what the hell we tryin' to figure out."

While we were talking, I peeped Sweets out the corner of my eye, aiming the shotty at the window, it startled me. I thought somebody was out there. "Sweets, what up! What you see?"

"Y'all need to saw this big-ass shotgun off," she said, wiping her tears with one of her sleeves.

The twins looked at me then back at her. I was as shocked as they were by her comment, she was serious.

"Hood, you hear this shit?" Mula said.

"This bitch trippin'," Bri said.

"What, what y'all think?" Sweets asked turning and waving the gun all wild and shit.

Everybody got the fuck out the way.

"Whoa! What the—" Moo yelled, avoiding the end of the barrel.

"Sweets, you right! You right!" I shouted, diving sideways onto the sofa.

"Bitch put the gun down. You buggin'!" Mula said.

She had run to the opposite corner of the room. Bri was on the floor, dying laughing.

Sweets said, "Oops, damn y'all—my bad."

Doe was down on one knee. He said, "You goddamn right that's yo' bad! Hood, get your damn friend!"

We all laughed and that was the first time we really grasped that iron. But, as you know, it wouldn't be our last.

K'ajji

Chapter 21

Zoo

"Hold—hol-up, y'all niggaz be the fuck quiet! I'm on the phone! Hel—hello. Hey Aunt Gwyn, this Zoo. I mean this, Chris. Yeah, I'm still in the hospital. I'm doing okay. It's a'ight, I know you had to work. Yeah, the doctor says about another week or two. Yeah, Auntie, I know I'm only sixteen. But—I—I'm not, I'm gon' stay in school, I promise. Ha—have you seen my momma? You ain't talked to her at all, too—yeah, I've been callin' home all day. She was supposed to have come back up here this morning but she never made it. Yeah, but visiting hours over at 9:00, and its 7:45. Okay, I'll keep tryin', too. Love you, bye," Zoo said and slammed the phone down. "Fuck ma! Where you at?"

"You gon' call the whole city? Nigga, yo' mufuckin' momma a'ight. Stop worryin' so damn much. She probably somewhere with Dexter. Shit nigga, yo' momma look good!"

"Fuck you, Trell! What I tell you about speakin' on her, huh? And who the fuck is Dexter?"

"Big-dick Dexter, nigga!" Trell said as everybody laughed.

"You ain't heard? That nigga got dick like a rope! Whatchu cryin' 'bout?" Tre-Rida asked with a Jamaican accent, mimicking Eddie Murphy's lines from his classic standup show *Raw*.

The crew was dying laughing.

"Fuck y'all niggaz!" Zoo said. "Y'all mommaz probably with 'em! If my leg wasn't broke, y'all know!"

U-Tee said, "Aw nigga if yo' leg wasn't broke, what? You ain't gon' do shit."

Lil' Zoo smiled, it was just a show for the big homie, though. He was still worried inside. It wasn't like his mother to not show when she said she was going to do something. Not hearing from her had him on edge, especially in the position he was in. Lil' Trell, Tre-Rida, E-Class, U-Tee, and Proof had been at the hospital keeping him, Famo, Blue, and the lil' chics from the hood company all day. Zoo's lil' bitch, Goodie, had just left, or at least they thought she had left. They were all in his room, fucking with him for the time being, when Goodie walked back into the room. She was carrying *Get Well* balloons and a huge gift-wrapped present in royal blue paper and topped with a black bow.

"Aww bae, I thought you was gone. You bought me some more shit?" Zoo asked with a smile. "You so sweet."

She dropped the box on the nightstand and let the balloons float to the ceiling. The scolding look on her face said she was unhappy about something. "What bitch you got sneakin' up here droppin' shit off as soon as you think I'm gone? The bitch probably saw my car out in the parkin' lot! That's why she didn't come up!"

"What, what you talkin' about?" Zoo questioned.

"You told me to leave my car and to have my momma come pick me up," Goodie replied. "Tell me why we left? We pulled out the parking lot and errything! Then I realized I'd left my purse! So, we turned around! I come back in the door downstairs and the nurse say some bitch had just dropped this shit off at the desk fo' yo' ass! I look at the card on this heavy-ass box and it say, *"From Win—Yet with love! Get well soon."* Well, let's see what the bitch brought you, shall we?"

Goodie picked up the box and heaved it onto the hospital bed. When it landed, the box's lid flew off. As it tumbled, a human head rolled out onto Zoo's lap, it was his mother's.

Goodie let out one of those white girl's screams, the kind only heard in horror movies.

"What tha—mommaaa!" Zoo yelled as his friends looked on, wincing and groaning.

Goodie cried for God as the nurses and police rushed into the room.

"Jeesusss!" she screamed and fell to her knees.

Chapter 22

J. L.

When J. L. got word that they'd found Chaka's decapitated corpse with fifty-two bullet wounds in it in an alley off 10th in Atkinson and that the day before her head was sent to his nephew as he laid in his hospital bed, he caught the next flight home. His heart was broken, his baby sister had nothing to do with the streets. The life he led had cost her hers, it was a message from Teague. The number of bullet wounds represented the count on the indictment. They'd found her body in the back of one of the old spots. Specifically, one of the first spots J. L. had ever run because Teague had handed him the keys to it to put some money in his pockets.

His past had truly come back to haunt him and in the worst way. Greed was still getting the best of him. Yet, he hadn't recognized it. If only he had paid the young niggas, his sister would still be alive. He should have known that leaving his family unprotected would end with fatal results. He was dealing with the bloodline of a stone-cold killer.

Now he was back home out at his crib off Layton by the airport. He had Po Kelly and Burleigh Rick by his side. He'd assigned Spree and Kane to guard his sister Genesis with their lives. She and Zoo were all he had left on his momma's side of the family. Lil' Zoo and the others were still at St. Joseph's out on 51st in Burleigh. He had them moved to Sinai Samaritan with niggas posted around the clock. So much had happened since he left, so much death. He had a lot of funeral arrangements to make.

"I thought y'all was gon' handle these lil' niggaz! It seems they've been handlin' us! I done lost my sister! And then we done lost damn near twenty niggaz! What the fuck goin' on?" he snapped at his henchmen.

Burleigh Rick said, "Shit, we sent some of the lil' homies over there. As you know, that didn't end well. It's like they knew we was comin'."

"How the fuck they know we was comin'? I called and ain't spoke to nobody but you about that inside info! Who you tell, nigga?"

"Shit, nobody besides Po and the lil' niggaz that was ridin', Lil' Zoo, Famo, and Blue, still—"

"Who you send over there?" J. L. asked, frustrated by his response.

"Clipse, Geom, Glitch, Lil' Brick, Brando, Fl—"

"Yeah, yeah. I'm talkin' niggaz that's still alive! Clipse, Brick, Black, and Glitch dead. Who that leave?"

"Geom, Brando, Fly, and Church. They over on the block now," Burleigh Rick replied.

"Well, get 'em together. Po, you know what to do. Take 'em to the basement. Don't kill 'em though. Find out if they told anybody. They know what go on over there. They see all that shit all over the walls. They'll talk if they know somethin'. We gotta get on top of this shit, fast!"

Chapter 23

Jahnahdah

11:45 p.m. - 3 Days Later

Greentree Apartments

Janahdah heard a knock at her door. She wasn't expecting Emma, Mona, and China for at least another half hour.

"Who is it?" she called out, still in front of her bathroom mirror, putting on her makeup. She waltzed out the bathroom towards the door. She heard another knock. "I told you, bitches, to give me forty-five minutes! Not te—" She flung open the door and stopped speaking when she saw Doe standing in her hallway. She finished her sentence, "—not ten. Doe, whatchu doin' here? You ain't say you was comin' over." Leaving the door open, she walked back towards the bathroom.

Doe welcomed himself in. "That's what it is, huh?" Doe said, watching all that ass wobble underneath the thin fabric that covered her body. "I see you all dressed. Where you goin'?" he asked, taking a seat in her living room, and making himself at home.

He picked up the remote and switched on the TV, swinging his feet up onto the coffee table.

"Out!" she yelled from the bathroom.

"With who?" he yelled back with a smile.

She came out of the bathroom. "Dang nosey, I know you ain't jealous. And get your damn, dirty-ass feet off my shit," she said as she knocked his feet off the table.

She walked into her bedroom and he followed.

Doe said, "I know you ain't about to go kick it with them stank hoes, China, Emma, and Mona tonight over me?"

"Oh—ooh, no you didn't just go in on my bitches like that! Don't nobody be sayin' shit about all them dusty-ass 3C niggaz you be with, runnin' round hollin, *"Threee! Traaayz! Three*

Chambers!" With they weak ass." She pointed out as she sat down at her vanity mirror.

"Ha-haaa, you got that one. I'll give you that. They far from dusty, though." Doe was admiring her beauty as she applied her eyeliner. He grabbed her hand before she could apply another stroke and whispered in her ear, "Nahdah, whatchu got on under there?" while kissing on her neck.

"Nothin', why?" she replied with a giggle.

"Come here, stand up, and let me see." She stood up and faced him, melting into his stare. She smelled so good. Doe tore the top of her Nicole Miller jumpsuit open, ravishing her breasts.

"Oooh! Ooooh, shit—baby—baby wa-wait. Let me-ooooh! Let me take it off!" she moaned as she wrapped her arms around his head.

"For what?" he mumbled as he continued to suck, nip and kiss her nipples. "I bought it, I'll buy this shit a thousand times over if I got to." He pushed her up against the wall, kissing her passionately as he continued to rip her clothing from her body.

He ripped and kissed, moving from her lips to her neck and down to her stomach. He tore her jumpsuit completely open and it now looked more like a cape hanging from her shoulders. He got on his knees, raised one of her thighs, placed it over his shoulder, and began to lick and suck on her clit. Then he pushed two fingers inside of her.

"Doe—Dooeee!" she whined as she discarded what was left of the jumpsuit hanging from her shoulders. She stood there in nothing but her Giuseppe stilts.

Doe put both her legs over his shoulders as he lifted her up and carried her to the bed, laying her on the edge of the bed, he practiced the alphabet between her thighs as he anticipated her letter, working his tongue.

She said, "Ooh, ooh shit! Ooohhh! D, oh, oh my! E. Doe, Doooeee! Eeeeeeee! Awwww-awww! Shit, I'm—I'm cummin'! Shit, you muthafuckaaa! Oooh!" Her stilts were pointing toward the ceiling as her body shook. "Thank youuu! Thank you, babyyy!" she cooed as he removed his clothing.

"Don't thank me yet. We just gettin' started," he told her, sliding into her love cave eight inches deep.

"Awwww shit, niggggaaa!" she panted.

Doe beat Jahnahdah's pussy up all night and all morning. Her girls called and banged on her door but all they heard were her moans of passion. She already knew when she talked to them they'd have a few choice words for her ass. Fuck them, they wouldn't have been able to move either with all that pipe in their asses. Now, as she stood butt-ass naked at the stove, cooking her man some breakfast, she felt he deserved it after the way he'd fucked her brains out. After he finished eating, shit, she wanted some more, and that's when it hit her.

Oh, hell no! Doe was still in her room. When she stormed in, he was still underneath the sheet naked. So, she went over to him, trying to slap him.

"Uh—uh, I'ma beat yo' ass!" she said as she smacked him.

He rolled off the other side of the bed, trying to get away from her. He grabbed the sheet and tried to cover up, but so did she. It became a tug-of-war.

"Jah, what the fuck you doin'?" he asked in confusion. She'd never hit him before.

"Nigga, you sucked the shit outta this pussy last night!" she said. "You don't even eat pussy! Who you been fuckin' with? I'm fuckin' you up! Who you been practicin' on, huh?"

Doe laughed and said, "Nahdah, you know I don't even get down like that girl. Stop playin' and let the sheet go." He was still smiling.

"Ain't!" she said, tugging angrily.

"Come on girl! Moo-Moo—"

"Moo-Moo my ass, nigga," she said. "You ain't gon' use him as no muthafuckin' decoy today! He ain't got no damn pussy!" She let the sheet go and grabbed the lamp on his ass.

"Nall, see—look—check it out! Nahdah, I ain't playin'. Don't throw that lamp at me!" he pleaded while wrapping himself in the sheet as if it was a bath towel. She was crying. His laughter had hurt her feelings. "Listen, I can explain," he protested.

Beep! Beep! Beeep! Beep! Beeep! Beeeep! Smoke detectors throughout the apartment began to sound off.

"Nahdah, girl you left the stove on! You lef—stop cryin'. Look, don't move," he said as he ran out the room towards the kitchen to put out the blaze, if necessary.

Luckily, that wasn't the case. Once he stopped the alarms, he returned to the bedroom carrying a skillet. The pancakes inside were as black as the skillet itself. He coughed and waved off some of the smoke which had drifted into the room. But Jahnahdah was sitting on the bed, knees pulled to her chest with her back resting against the headboard.

"You tryin' to kill us? I ain't eatin' this," Doe said, showing her the burnt flapjacks.

He opened the window and threw the entire skillet out of it. He left the window open and walked back over to her. But she still had her head down.

"Nahdah, bae, you think I'm cheatin'?" he asked as he sat down next to her and raised her chin.

"You don't just learn how to eat pussy in one day," she said. "I ain't stupid, nigga." She hung her head again.

"Aw, my name nigga now?" She sucked her teeth at him. "Nah, for real, listen. You got it all wrong. You know Moo just came home, right?"

"And, what that got to do with it?" she asked.

"Well, you know he got a million theories and stories about what the old heads put 'em up on while he was down. So, he tells me his big homie told 'em to run the ABC's on the clit, that every woman has her letter. And, that you can tell when you hit that joint cause she'll go crazy. I love you. So, I wanted my first experience to be with you," he explained and smiled as she looked up at 'em.

"Oh, yeah, what's my letter then, Doe?" she asked, finally showing a half-smile.

"As far as I can tell so far, it's 'E'." He leaned in and kissed her.

She said, "Aww bae, my stupid self." Smiling, she opened her arms to give him a hug.

"Nope woman!" he said. "That ain't gon' cut it! Give me some head! And you bet not know whatchu doin'."

She laughed. "Okay, I'll try. Just tell me how to do it."

They fucked and sucked each other into midday. Doe had some business he needed to take care of so after he was fed and showered up, he left. As he walked out of the apartment complex he felt good, like a new man. It's that feeling a nigga feels in his soul after getting some fie pussy. Jahnahdah had him on cloud nine. She had his heart wide open. She had him so fucked up that he was slipping. His head, his heart, and his eyes could've been left open on the pavement — literally. Because he never noticed Po sitting right there in the parking lot, watching him jump into the M.C.

K'ajji

Chapter 24

Hood

It was still hot out and me and the P.Y.T.'s were trying to enjoy the last few days of the good weather we had left and, although my brothers told me to stay off the block, and not to cross 12th in Burleigh, I did it anyway. Shit, we were walking and strutting our shit. We had on our lil' shorts with the shirts we'd just gotten made. On the back of them, it read *If It Ain't Rough It Ain't Me*. On the right sleeve was *P.Y.T.* and on the front and middle were our nicknames in large cursive letters. All types of niggas were trying to stop and holla. We just knew we were looking too good!

We hit 32nd in Burleigh and it was poppin' hard. All the hustlers were posted on the corners, stuntin' in their lil' jewelry. They had Donks, 'Lacs, trucks, and all kinds of shit parked out there. I mean, don't get me wrong, niggas from the deck had it going on, too. But we see them every day. Plus, Moe and Doe made sure it was clear we were off limits! Since I'm the oldest and the thickest of the squad, I gained the most attention. I was fucking them up!

My ass said, "Wham!" and titties said, "Bam!"

As we strolled through that bitch I couldn't do nothin' but catch and here we go. Got me one!

"Say, say—say, baby! You in the front!" Tre-Rida yelled from across the street.

At first, we kept it moving as if we didn't hear them. Then we heard one nigga say, "Nigga. fuck that bitch! You stay hoe huntin'."

Tre said, "Nigga be cool. Stop cock blockin'. Aye, slow down!" He jogged down on me and stopped me.

He was fine as hell, too; light-skinned nigga about 6'5, with naturally curly hair. I could tell he did this shit all the time. He was just too smooth.

"What up, baby girl? What's your name?" He spoke with his hands like he was already caressing a bitch.

"Tasha," I replied, still walking.

"Tasha, I'm Tre-Rida. You got a man? That must be him you reppin' on yo' shirt. Who is 2Hood? I don't know that nigga."

"Never mind all that. Nall, I ain't got no man."

"Damn!" he said. "Bad as you is! How old you is?"

"Old enough," I said. "Why, what up?"

"Shit, I'm just wonderin' if a nigga could give you a call sometimes. Maybe I can fuck with you."

"We can talk," I said. "Give me your number, I' ll hit you up," I told the crew to keep on walking while I got his information.

They were blocks away by the time he was through running his G. Then he offered me a ride to catch up with them. He was trying to show off one of his new toys. He had a black Jeep and it was nice. Everything was leather on the inside. It was real comfortable. I jumped out happy I had made a new friend. We kept strolling hood to hood. Everything was everything! That is, until Doe and Moo rode down on us on 27th in Capitol. They were about ten cars deep, all tinted, flexin'!

When they stopped, I threw my hands up. I'm like, "What up!" I didn't know who they were at first. I thought they were just some more niggaz trying to holler.

Moo jumped out of one of the cars in the middle of the caravan with a thumper in his hand. I'm thinking, what the fuck is he going to do with that gun?

"What the fuck we tell yo' ass!" he yelled, scanning our surroundings. "Getcha ass in the car!" he demanded. I didn't protest. He told Mula, Bri, Karma, and Lue, "I should make y'all ass keep walkin'! Out here with y'all shit all up y'all asses! Get y'all lil' ass in one of the cars behind us! And hurry the fuck up!"

My bitches didn't protest either, wisely. They clowned our asses to the fullest. We were so fucking embarrassed. Luckily, there weren't too many people out there. Thank God there was no one out there we knew, with their hating asses. They took every number we'd gotten from each and every one of us. The funny thing is, they gave us certain numbers back and told us to call and holla at the niggas. The trick was that we could only tell the niggas what they wanted us to tell them. The power of the pussy is as deadly as any knife or gun, and sharper than a two-edged sword. Believe me, you'll soon see.

***

Sweets

Look, it was all supposed to be a tactic to see what he'd do. But all the late-night calls between me and T-Dog had gotten to me. I mean, he was talking all that freaky shit to me. My hormones got out of control. I know I wasn't supposed to do, or say, shit that the twins hadn't put me up to. My assignment was to try to find out what he, Goldie, and the others were on. But instead of me reporting everything back like I was supposed to, I kept our creeping a secret for a little while. I knew Hood wouldn't have approved of it.

See, T-Dog and every nigga off A.T.K. to 3C knew how the twins felt about niggas fucking with us, especially older niggas. I knew Hood would have said, *"He too old to be fuckin' on you!"* But shit, I was tired of watching Playboy and playing the finger-fucking and titty-sucking game with niggas my age. This nigga was talking about giving it to me right! Plus, I was curious and my momma was always home. However, I knew somebody's momma who was the total opposite. I needed a partner in crime. Mrs. Hines worked and worked and worked some more. So, I talked Bri into letting T-Dog and Ready come through and fuck with us one night. That one night turned into every time her momma worked third shift. That's how Bri ended up falling in love with Ready Reed.

***

Brianna

Hold up, bitch. Let me holla at 'em. You tellin' all my business. Yeah, I fell in love with the nigga, but bullshit ain't about nothing! My momma didn't even know I was fucking! She took me to the

doctor to get my six-month checkup and come to find out I got gon-
orrhea! That's right, the muthafuckin' clap! This bitch done zapped
me! And do you know we caught this nigga downtown coming out
of B-Boy Trends and he tried to act like he didn't know me. I guess
it was because he was with this hoe-bitch named Tameera. I tried to
fuck his ass up! That's when everything came to light. The entire
crew was with me.

"Ready, what's up, nigga?" I asked. "I see you ain't been an-
swerin' my pages."

He didn't say shit. He tried to keep on steppin'. They gave us
their backs, walking in front of us.

I said, "Yeeaahhh, you know you burnt me, bitch!" I ran and
jumped, swinging as hard as I could.

As he turned around, I caught him in his ear. He tried to run up
on me, but Mula stepped in front of him. Then the nigga had the
nerve to call me out of my name. I was trying to get to his ass again
when Sweets grabbed me.

Hood said, "Hold on! What the fuck goin' on? Ready, you been
fuckin' my sistah, nigga? Huh, huh?" She ran up on him and two-
pieced his ass. *Boom! Boom!* "Now bust a muthafuckin' move," she
said. "I dare you! The twins will be to see yo' hoe-ass! You can bet
that!"

Tameera didn't move or say a word. I guess she knew we would
have torn her ass up. We walked off.

"I wanna kill that nigga!" I yelled out of frustration. I was hurt
and humiliated.

I felt stupid because at the time I felt I still loved him. Next, we
told the twins and they went over there and checked the shit out of
Ready and T-Dog. But since they were already at war with those
Zoo niggas, they let them breathe. They also checked me and
Sweets. "Then let's just say they started setting examples for what
they'd done, why they did it, and why they said what they said."

"Talk to'em Bri!"

"I got'em Mu."

Chapter 25

Bri
First Blood

10:38 p.m.

This nigga named E-Class drove down on us on 18th in Locust. He had given Mula his number that day the twins clowned us. She'd been putting him off for weeks because of them. But tonight, she and Sweets were supposed to be hooking up with him and his man, Geom on 34th in G-Street which is short for Galena. Apparently, that's where they thought Mula lived with her auntie. Unfortunately, they were in for a helluva surprise and so were we.

When Class and Geom pulled up the block was unusually quiet. Yeah, it was semi—late, but it seemed they were the only niggas out that night which was strange to Geom. They pulled up in front of the grey and white house and checked the address, then they pulled off.

"Mannn, you sure about this shit," Geom asked in a strained voice as he passed the weed to Class.

"Yeah, nigga, I'm telling you the bitch, Pam straight." He blew out his smoke. "All her lil' buddies bad. You can't lose nigga Whichever one she plugs you with you str-straight, nigga," Class replied, taking the last few draws of the weed between his nubs.

"I ain't talkin' 'bout that fool-ass nigga. I'm talkin' about it bein' a muthafuckin' ghost town out here. And these bitches talkin' 'bout pullin' around in the alley?"

"Nigga, we straight with yo' scary ass. You can thank me for the pussy after we get it."

They turned into the alley and pulled behind the house. They parked and got out of the car. Geom pulled his burner out of the waistband of his pants. The house was lit up and they could hear music coming from inside.

"I told you, nigga," Class said. "Them hoes in there partyin'. Come on, put that shit up. You gon' scare the pussy off."

Reluctantly, Geom tucked the .9mm into his waistband. They walked up to the back door and Class banged on it as hard as he could so he could be heard over the loud music. However, we were outside in the bushes, watching their every move. Mula answered the door in nothing but her t-shirt and panties, acting like she was drunk.

"Heyyy! Heyyy Class! Wha-what took y'all so long?" she greeted them. "Come on in!"

Once they walked in, we shot around to the front door and came inside. In the back hallway, Class looked back at Geom as they both watched Mula sashay up a small flight of steps that led to a door and into the kitchen.

"Told you!" Class mouthed with a smile.

They gave each other a pound. As soon as they stepped foot through that door — they were dead! They walked into the kitchen and Doe was standing there with two .357s in their faces. Geom had made a move to reach for his waistband, changing his mind when he felt the barrel of the *K* pressed against the back of his head. Moo had crept out the basement and was behind them.

"Shit!" Geom cursed underneath his breath.

Whodini's anthem, *Friends* was put on pause.

"Take they guns, Mula," Doe barked with an evil grin on his face. "Y'all niggaz thought y'all was about to get y'all some pussy. Um, um, umm, y'all done fucked up!" he said as Mula relieved them of their straps.

"Sure, the fuck did, stupid niggaz," Moo said, shaking his head. "Hood, Lue, Sweets and Bri get y'all asses in here!"

We came out of the living room with guns in hand. Geom had his hands to the sky.

He looked over at Class with a frown and said, "I knew I shouldn't of listened to yo' ass!"

"Shut the fuck up, nigga, and turn y'all ass around!" Moo said. "Slowly!"

"We goin' in the basement," Doe said.

That's when they realized they were in trouble. Geom tried to get on some tough shit. "I ain't goin' nowhere!" Geom said. "Y'all gon' have to do what y'all gotta do right here!" He was hoping this was a simple robbery.

Moo put the muzzle of his chopper to his forehead. "You know that ain't no problem, right?" Moo said. "Hood, pump that shit back up!"

When she turned to do so, Geom had a change of heart. "Waiiittt! A'ight!" Geom yelled. "Damn, what the fuck y'all want anyway?"

Doe said, "We'll talk about all that when we get where we goin' potna!"

They led them at gunpoint down into the basement.

Once there, Moo told them, "Walk to the back and stand against that brick wall. Then turn around and face us."

Class finally got the balls to speak, "Com—come on man. So—so what y'all want?" He was spooked.

Doe laughed. "Ha-haaaa! That's funny, nigga. See, ya man Geom know what it is. Don't cha G? I just assumed you did, too. You should. Ya man here is one of the few that got away a few weeks ago when niggaz came on 3 Chambers and shot up the crib. Shit, both of y'all Zoo, right? We was for either one of y'all. Class, you brought us a bonus. For that, we appreciate you. We ain't gotta go lookin' for this nigga."

We were standing in the back behind the twins. So, when they both stepped aside and Doe said, "Go ahead, Y'all kill these niggaz."

I was shocked! Lue, our youngest was scared. Shit, I think we all were.

Hood said, "What! Wait a minute! Y'all ain't say—"

Moo cut her off mid-sentence. "These muthafuckaz is the same niggaz flashin' on us every chance they get! If we let 'em go, they damn sure comin' for y'all ass! Y'all need to know and understand how serious this shit is! While y'all runnin' around this muthafucka, hollin at niggaz, y'all not knowin' who the enemy is. This game is cold! Hood, the nigga, Tre-Rida? Yeah, him too! We took that number outta yo' fuckin' pocket! Now, what y'all gon' do? We about to go up here and turn this music back up. When we come back down here, niggaz better be dead in this bitch! No bullshit!"

Doe said, "All y'all better bust y'all gunz, too. Y'all hollin' y'all sistahs and talkin' that P.Y.T. shit. Loyalty is everything. Shitz real. Do I gotta call Wintress, Yetta, or Bella G to show y'all how to—"

A tear rolled down Hood's cheek. She put her finger to his lips. "He right, y'all," Hood said. "These niggaz got to go. Go head, blast that shit. When y'all come back, it'll be done." She looked each one of us in our eyes.

"Waaaiiittt!" Class cried out, trying to plead his case.

Clack! Claaack! Sweets cocked the sawed-off. She said, "Get right with God, niggaz."

The twins left, we all slowly raised our guns. Of course, Class and Geom begged us not to shoot but it was too late for them. At the sound of the old school classic, *I Heard It Through the Grapevine,* we let go bodyin' them, niggas.

Chapter 26

Doe

11:50 p.m.

When I drove down Teutonia and turned onto Green Street into the apartment complex, blueberry and cherry lights were flashing everywhere. Shit, I couldn't even get into the parking lot I wanted. So, I pulled into the parking lot of the apartment building next to it and jumped out of the car. Both parking lots were packed with nosey neighbors.

What the fuck's going on here? I thought to myself as I hit the alarm. I made it through the crowd and jogged across the street to the adjacent lot. I posted up, trying to see what happened. Standing next to an old man, I asked, "You know anything about what happened?"

"I ain't sure," he said. "Hell, they say somebody done jumped on some young lady that stay in there." He pointed at the building.

"Aw, for real?" I said, moving closer to see if I could spot my baby amongst the onlookers.

I saw her car was parked in its usual spot. Mona's shit was parked right next to it. So, I just knew they had to be out here somewhere. It wasn't until the police started yelling for everybody to move back that I realized something was seriously fucked up.

"Move!"

"Everybodyyy clear out! We need to clear a path to the ambulance!" another officer yelled.

When the glass doors opened and the EMT's rushed out with the stretcher, I heard her name. My heart dropped. Emma, Mona, and China were running beside the emergency personnel.

I ran over to the stretcher. "Jahnahdah!Jah! Oh my God, I'm here! Oh, my fuckin' God!"

Mona cried as they wheeled her toward the ambulance.
By the time I got to her, they had an oxygen mask over her face, squeezing air into her lungs.

I reached for her hand and grabbed it. "Nahdah! Jahnahdah, baby!"

She was unrecognizable. *How could this be?* I thought to myself as tears flooded my eyes.

"Step to the side, sir! Please, let us do our jobs," the paramedic pleaded.

"Is she gon' be okaaayyy? Is she gon' make it?" China fell to her knees.

Emma was in shock. I grabbed her and shook her. "Em, what happened?" She just looked at me. "Emma, talk to me! What the fuck happened to Jahnahdah?"

"I don't know," she said. "We—we was knockin' at her door. We heard screams and shit breakin'. Then—then some dude came runnin' out. He—he knocked all three of us down
and kept on runnin'. Oh, my God! Doe—Doe it—it's so much blood. She wasn't breathin'!" she cried.

"Come on, bitch!" China yelled.

"Just two!" one of the EMT's shouted.

"China, you and Mona go!" I ordered. "We'll meet y'all at the hospital!" Mona climbed in and they slammed the ambulance door. I asked Emma, "Did y'all see what he looked like?" She was frozen in time. The siren from the ambulance started up as they pulled off. Emma just stared into the distance. "Emma, did y'all see what the nigga looked like?" Again, she just looked at me. "Fuck, come on!" I grabbed her hand and walked her to my car.

My mind was everywhere. I'm in traffic with a banger on my lap, doing 90 mph. Within minutes I was swinging and dipping into the hospital parking lot. Niggas knew my heart. It was a mistake I should have seen coming a mile away. As soon as I stopped, Emma jumped out, and then I heard her scream. When I looked up all I saw was the chrome. Po Kelly stood behind it. Then flash! The nigga blasted me and Emma leaving us for dead.

Chapter 27

Hood

When I heard my brother had gotten shot, I damn near passed the fuck out. It hadn't even been an hour and a half earlier when we had committed our first murders. We had dropped everybody else off on G-Street. We were actually just getting ready to mash out with two bodies in the trunk when Jilla pulled up and gave Moo the news. I caught the ass-end of the conversation. My mind was still on how we'd blazed those boys like a firing squad. So, at first, I wasn't paying any attention until I saw Moo's body language change.

He said, "What! When! He was jus—"

"Calm down. Listen, don't go to the hospital right now. That's how they caught 'em slippin'. Emma gone. He and Jah are critical up in ICU," Jilla called himself trying to whisper as he leaned into the car, but I heard his ass.

I said, "What! Whatchu just say?"

"Hood, jus—just be cool, a'ight?" Moo tried to calm me down, but I wasn't hearing that shit.

"Hell nall! Fuck that! Did he just say—did you just say Doe in the ICU? What happened? Moozeere, don't you keep this shit from me! What happened?"

Moo gripped the steering wheel, banging his head against it a few times. He said, "Fuck! Fuck! Fuuccckkk! Domaaain! How you let these niggaz—" When he sat back tears soaked his face. He took a deep breath and looked at me. "He got shot five times." I started sobbing real hard. "Jilla, make sure he stays safe until we can get to 'em. I gotta—we gotta handle this business real quick," he said. "You hear anything else, call me."

Jilla just nodded, jumped back into his car, and stabbed out.

Moo grabbed my shoulder as my head rested against the passenger side window. "You gotta be strong, Hood. I need you," he said as we pulled off. I couldn't stop crying, even while we were dumping the bodies. I was going through it. "Come on, Hood! Grab the nigga's legs!" Moo whispered in a hushed but demanding tone.

I felt weak like I could barely move. We were a few blocks over on 32nd in McKinley, in an alley. We were standing at the trunk of the car which was wide open.

I said, "I can't—I jus—"

"Girl, you wanna go to muthafuckin' prison, huh? Cause that's exactly where we goin' if we get caught with these two dead fuck niggaz! Now grab his mutha—fuckin—legs! Don't start gettin' all queazy on me and shit."

I grabbed Geom's legs and we flung his ass out the trunk and behind somebody's garage. After doing the same with Class, we jumped into the car and hit it!

Moo said, "Listen, I been thinkin' I want you to wait a few days and then call that nigga, Tre-Rida. Just see how he talkin'. Feel 'em out. Matter fact, call that nigga today."

"But I wanna go see, Doe!"

"You can't go see 'em."

"What the fuck you mean?"

"Hood, if they watchin' they'll know you either family or a friend. We can't have dat. Just do what I tell you. Doe gon' be a'ight. He's my twin, I feel it. We gotta stay focused on our next move. If we're vulnerable, we die. They'll crush us. You gotta be a soulja.

"I want you to go to school as if nothing is different like everything is normal. The only difference is, I want you to keep the hammer on you at all times, keep it cocked 'n ready. I'll keep a few niggaz in the shadows but never depend on another mufucka to bust. When it's on, it's all on you. Dead niggaz learn that the hard way. Don't tell Mula 'nem if they ain't already heard. You don't wanna scare 'em, but I want all y'all to keep them tools close.

"Use your instincts. Jilla said some nigga went out to Jahnahdah's crib and beat her half to death. I told bro' to stop always bein' seen with that girl out in public if he loved her. But he wasn't tryin' to hear me. As a woman, you gotta know the power of the pussy, sis. You see how niggaz fell for the pussy trap last night? Got they ass stretched? As you see, now they used the same tactic to get Doe. You see it?"

"Yeah, Moo, I see it."

"Well, it's time to use it to your advantage. It all comes down to who's the best at this shit. The game don't discriminate. They killed Emma. You ready? I need to know—"

"Yeah, Moo." I looked him straight in the eyes. "I'm ready."

K'ajji

Chapter 28

Moo

3 Days Later

Now that bruh was laid up in the hospital, it was hard for me to focus. But I had to put my emotions to the side and lead 3C. The only question that remained was would they allow me to do so? Doe was always on some *we shit* when it came down to it. I chose to play the back and let him do his thing. Their camaraderie was something they'd established while I was doing time so the bond was different.

Yeah, we're identical. We feel the same on many subjects. However, we're still two different niggas. This is something they'd have to learn and quickly. I consider myself a connoisseur. My tolerance for bullshit didn't exist.

I pulled up on Hadley where we'd decided to meet and discuss our next move. I'd been there earlier putting everything together. But I had to go grab the last pieces to my plan. I'd heard Gina had been patrolling the area heavy, looking for me. She knew for a fact that with Doe being shot, it meant I was on business. She'd been all up at the hospital and shit. From what I heard, she'd just missed me as I got up out of there.

Bruh was out of surgery for the moment. They still weren't sure if he was going to make it because they weren't able to reach all the slugs. He still hadn't come to. However, Jahnahdah was getting better as each day passed. Tip, Fry, Mona, and China stayed out there. Jahnahdah's brothers, Eric, and Davin flew out there with their mother. They were all stayin' downtown at the Hilton.

Her brothers wanted to get down, but I asked them to chill. I told them once I pinpointed the nigga responsible, I'd holla. So, I asked if they'd lay low until then. Tank, Jilla, Smoke, and some more 3C niggas was out there scattered about. It was a must that everybody out at the hospital was kept safe. Therefore, that left me with a small army to deal with. But fuck it, we'd have to make do.

As I stepped into the spot, Bella, Wintress, and Yetta greeted me with hugs. They had tears in their eyes.

"What up twin?" Yetta asked, holding me a lil' longer than the others did.

They hadn't seen me in a minute because the same morning Doe got hit, I went nuts with the *K* on some dolo shit, broad day stretching shit.

"Shit, y'all already know what time it is," I said. "We ain't dead yet, baby." Everybody was dressed in killa attire.

Looking around, Block, Freaky, and Six hadn't made it yet. So, I hollered at one of the lil' ones, "Crook, where the fuck yo' brotha Block and Freak at?"

He said, "They should be on they way now. You said nine, right?"

"Yeah, you right," I said. "It's 9:01 now. We'll wait, though. Everybody that ain't guarding the hospital needs to be here. I thought I'd made that clear."

So we waited all thirty-two of us. Thirty minutes rolled by then forty-five. An hour and fifteen minutes later, these niggas walk in. Everybody stood up.

"Damn, glad to see y'all niggaz could join us," I said, looking at the Rolex. "Y'all know this meeting was scheduled for nine, right?"

Block stepped forward to speak for all three of them, saying, "Yeah, maaannn, we got caught up with these bitches—"

Boommm! I upped foe-foe and put his noodles on the wall. "Anybody else wanna talk about bitches while my brotha laid up in the hospital with five muthafuckin' bullet holes in his chest? Six? Freak?" They didn't say shit.

They just fell in their six with everybody else. I tucked the Bull.

"A'ight then, let's get to it. Relax, I'll take care of this myself later on. I know y'all ain't used to me callin' it. And by all means, I wouldn't be had it been my choice. This position belongs to my brother and I ain't him. But, in so many ways, to know him is to know me. I'm the closest entity to 'em.

"However, I've been places he's never been, seen things I'll hope 'til I die that he'll never see. Now he shot up, fightin' for his life. I read this quote while I was in the joint. It was written by a great author named Shannon Holmes. I took it to heart. I now, wholeheartedly, utter those very words to y'all. *I take lead, follow me. If I cross you, kill me.*

"Right now, I'm askin' for everything y'all gave my brotha, and hopefully, y'all have given each other over the years. I ask for your love, your allegiance, and your hands in malignity. Now, if you with me, let me see the treyz!" To my surprise, everybody threw them up.

Telesis threw 'em up and said, "Treeey-Ceee! Moo-Mooo, babyyy reppin' 3C to the fullest."

"A'ight!" I said. "It's drama time." I snatched off the blanket I'd covered the table with earlier, revealing the arsenal of weapons that lay beneath. "As y'all can see, we have guests. Some of you already know my sistah, Hood. Standin' next to her is Sweets, Bri, and Mula. I see that look in some of y'all eyes. It's all on y'all faces. They're young and beautiful. You may think they ain't built for this. Don't let the pretty faces fool you.

"They'll bust them thangz, trust me. And I tell you, a niggaz worse downfall is his lust for pussy. At times, it's his love for it. In turn, it'll become our instrument, our intaglio beneath the surface to touch 'em. Yetta, Wintress, Honesty, and Telesis, no doubt y'all already know. Y'all beautiful as well, but chances are niggaz done seen y'all around and know y'all from the hood. With that said, we gotta be careful.

"Tonight, we goin' for the body since the snake been tuckin' his head. Word is Burleigh Rick has been real arrogant like he can't be touched. My sources say that he stays his fat ass up in one of they dope houses, eatin', and getting' money." I smiled. "Well, we gon' hit 'em where it hurt. We goin' in, takin' everything, and killin' everybody. Yetta, I'm takin' you, Hood, Mula, Sweets, and Telesis." I saw disappointment in some of the other soulja's eyes.

Wintress sucked her teeth. Brianna was visibly upset as well. "Everybody just be cool. The opportunity will arise. Believe me, y'all a get y'all chances to flash shit down. Telesis ain't goin' in."

"Damn, Moo!" she whined.

I pulled a black duffel bag from underneath the table and sat it down. They were all confused when I pulled out the Domino Pizza outfit. Then I slid five hockey masks and five blank jumpsuits across the table and said, "Ladies, I need y'all to show sis 'nem how to wrap up. It's Friday the 13th!"

Chapter 29

Goldie

Earlier That Week

It's a dirty game but you just got to know how to play it. You know I had to show my face at the hospital in an attempt to show good faith. Me, Prince, Ready, and T-Dog slid through there. That's when I ran into Moo. I fed the nigga the sympathy-empathy speech as if I wished Doe the best. When really, I could give a fuck whether the nigga lived or died. Shit Po and Ross fucked up anyway, popping the nigga in his chest.

They know damn well headshots are what gets the job done. When I gave them niggas the info on Jahnahdah, I expected an execution. Instead, here I am playing the role of the sad visitor. I'm good, though. Ha-haaa! A nigga even orchestrated a few tears. See, my plan is simple. There can only be one king.

So, while pulling J.L.'s coat to the shit, the twins are on, such as their whereabouts, etc., I figured why not kill a few birds with one stone and give the twins some shit to run with as well. Yeah, I know what you thinking, dirty, snake, back-biting-ass nigga. Yeah, fuck you too! All these niggas are in the way. So, I pulled Moo to the side.

He said, "Goldie, I appreciate you comin'. That was good shit how you looked out and told us what ol' girl said 'bout niggaz tryin' to come through as well. You gave us the heads ups."

"Yeah, homeboy. Anytime. Hear me? Now, you know I came as soon as I heard. How he doin'?"

"We don't know. The doctor says as soon as things change for the better or worse, they'll let us know."

"Damn, how many times he get hit?" I asked, already knowing the answer. I could feel his pain and I enjoyed it.

"Five times, man," he replied, holding his head.

"Doe, my muthafuckin' nigga!" I put on a show. I said, "You know if you need me, or any of my—" I pushed out the tears.

"Nah, we good. We'll handle these niggaz. Good look, though. This ain't y'all war."

"Well, at least let me leave you with this. You know I make a lot of moves and fucks with a lot of niggaz, right?"

"For sure."

"One of the niggaz I be hittin' on consignment got at me this morning cause he heard what happened. He knows I fucks with y'all heavy and whatnot. Well, Ride say he real close to one of them Zoo niggaz. I believe he say the nigga name JiVontre."

"You talkin' 'bout Tre-Rida?"

"I don't know. Could be, but I ain't sure. It very well could be. But anyway, lil' buddy say JiVontre got a real hatred for the nigga, Burleigh Rick. Say Burleigh Rick supposedly pistol-whipped the young boy cause he was short a few thou on some bricks. Gave the lil' nigga three hundred stitches.

"He got to ramblin' off at the mouth about Burleigh Rick's habits. Say the njgga be at this spot over on 28th in Locust like 24/7, talkin' shit and swallowin' spit. He collectin' that cash with a few more niggaz. It supposed to be somethin' major over there. Gave me the address and everythang." I handed Moo the address I had cuffed in the palm of my hand.

As I stood to leave, the look in his eyes told me the rest. "We go way back, nigga. A.T.K.!" I said.

He said, "That's home forever. Nothin' can ever change that. Again, I'm appreciative. I'll be sure to pay Burleigh Rick's bitch-ass a visit."

I'm thinking in my head, *I know you will.*

Chapter 30

Mula

4 Nights Later

Dressed like Jason Voorhees with two nines in my hand, Hood, Sweets, and I stood watch over five niggaz as they lay on the floor with their hands bound behind their backs. Moo and Yetta were ransacking the house, looking for the money and the dope. It's crazy how a sexy bitch in a Domino's hat and uniform gained us all access. Telesis made it look so easy! Hold up, though! Let me bring it back so y'all can envisage this shit.

1:21 a.m.

The red brick house sat alone in the middle of the block on a grassy knoll. The porch wasn't well-lit which was perfect to obscure the invasion. We moved up the steps quickly, ducking just below the sight of the window lines. In the stillness of the night, we lurked. Hood and I were on one side, Moo, Yetta, and Sweets on the other side of the door. Telesis pulled up in the stolen pizza delivery truck to do her thing. She casually grabbed two hot pizzas and walked up the steps. She rang the doorbell. We heard movement inside as we pressed ourselves against the building's siding. Lesis pulled her hat low.

"Who is it?" a male voice called from the other side of the door.

"Domino's," Telesis said in a diminutive voice that could barely be heard. Logic opened the door, gun in hand.

"Who? Ain't nobody." But as he thought about it, Burleigh Rick's fat ass just may have ordered this shit.

"Domino's," she repeated with a smile, giving him sex appeal. He couldn't help but notice all the cleavage she was showing, how her lil' blue pants hugged her thighs and her pussy print.

"Damn, oh! Aw shit! Never mind this." He tucked his gun.

He was admiring her beauty as well as looking over his shoulder to make sure nobody else was coming. He didn't want to share this precious gem he thought he'd found. Opening the screen door, he crept out onto the porch. "Damn babyyy! Who is you?" That's when Moo stepped from the cover of darkness. He startled the young hustler. "Oh shit!" He jumped.

"Shhhhh!" Moo whispered, putting the barrel of his gun to his lips. "Don't say shit, just blink. Understand?" He nodded yes. "How many niggaz in the house? Is that six? Nod yes or no, nigga! Yo' ass blinkin' too fast. How many, six?" He nodded yes, again as Lesis took his gun from his waistband and walked back to the truck. She pulled down the block. "A'ight, turn around, nigga." As he turned, we stepped out of the shadows. His eyes got big. I guess he realized it wouldn't end well. "If you make a sound, yo' momma gon' be sick about you. Walk."

Using Logic as a shield, Moo led us in with guns up. Yetta and I were on one side of him and Hood and Sweets on the other side. The living room was empty as far as anything breathing. There was just burgundy furniture, wood floors, and white walls. On the dining room table old KFC chicken buckets, pizza boxes, McDonald's cups, and wrappers were strewn about. Also, empty and half-empty liquor and soda bottles literally covered the table. These niggas were nasty. To our left was a staircase. Sweets covered it with Shotty as planned. Voices could be heard coming from the kitchen. Yetta watched our backs, covering the living room with the Mac. As we stepped into the kitchen, everybody had their backs to us as they weighed, cut, and bagged the product.

Moo pushed Logic to the floor and yelled, "What up niggaz!" He had gained their attention.

"Oh, shit!" one of them yelled, trying to reach.

Boc! Boc! Boc! Boc! Boc! I let the nines bark, laying him down. The rest quickly surrendered.

"Don't shoot! Don't shoot!" rang out as one of the workers declared peace.

I stared at him in silence and slowly cocked my head to the side as if I didn't understand boss plea. As smoke oozed out of the barrels of Nina Simone and Millie Jackson, a feeling I couldn't explain came over me. The head movement was a scare tactic. I'd seen Jason do it countless times after he'd slaughter his victims. After disarming them we laid their asses down in the living room.

Moo said, "I guess we just missed that fat muthafucka, Rick! Where the rest of that shit at? And don't everybody speak at one time." Silence. "Awe, y'all think I'm playin'. Think we bullshittin', huh?" He grabbed a half-empty 7-Up bottle off the dining table and walked over to the captives. Screwing off the top, he stuck the barrel of his gun inside the mouth of the 2-liter, put it to Logic's head and pulled the trigger. He blew his brains all over the dudes who laid beside him in both directions. Then—they all wanted to talk.

"I—I—I don't knowww, I swear I don't knooowww! This my first daaay!" That's one.

"Upstaaairs! That shit upstaaairs!" another one yelled. That's two.

It's in the boxes of Baby Wipes stacked under the bathroom sink and in the closet! The rest of the money is in the deep freezer in the basement! Maaan pleeease! I got kids! Pleeease!" The third nigga told it all.

Moo tapped Yetta on the shoulder and nodded towards the kitchen. He sent her down in the basement to grab the money while he went upstairs for the dope, which brings us back to the beginning of this shit. Hood, Sweets, and I stood watch over the five niggaz. Yetta brought two duffel bags filled with cash. Moo came downstairs with the dope.

Moo said, "A'ight, it's time. Flash on them bitch niggaz, P.Y.T. We out."

Moo and Yetta made their way to the front door as we dumped and pumped their bodies with metallic as we calcinated and ignited their souls while leaving cavities in their backs. I couldn't help but wonder about the difference between life and death. What we once feared no longer existed. So, it seemed. Gunfire was now a sound that we embellished.

K'ajji

Chapter 31

Hood

Back at the spot on Hadley, me and mine sat on the couch in silence as Yetta, Wintress, Telesis, and Honesty counted the take. Moo and some of the other 3C members were breaking down the weapons we'd just used and dumping them into acid. They had buckets full of the shit. They'd taken the jumpers and masks we'd worn and burned them. Moo's eyes were squinted, forehead wrinkled, and a cigarette dangled from his lips as I watched his every move. I was taking it all in. He looked up, caught me staring, and paused. Damn, my brother had changed.

"Hood, what up, you a'ight?" he asked, dumping his ashes. All eyes were now on me.

"Yeah, I'm good," I said. "Is you a'ight? When you start smokin' those?" I frowned.

"This just somethin' I do after I smoke weed." He looked at the squad. "P.Y.T., y'all straight?"

Mula said, "Shit, we just waitin' on 'em to get done countin' that money. My palms itchin'. I want some of that shit."

"Mulaaa!" I yelled, laughing. I was amazed by her statement and her boldness. Well, I shouldn't have been. Shit, true dat!

"What!" she said. "Girrrl, shit! You see all that money?"

Moo laughed. "Relax, y'all did all the work. Y'all a get y'all cut. I'm proud of y'all, too. Y'all handled y'all selves well, didn't hesitate."

There was a light knocking at the door. It sounded like a hundred guns were cocked simultaneously. Holding a K, Tank peeked out the curtain.

"Y'all chill!" he said. "It's just Smoke." He opened the door.

Smoke came in dressed in fatigues, black jeans, and boots, breathing harder than a muthafucka. He couldn't even talk.

"Damn lil' nigga, What up? Talk to us."

Smoke was so out of breath he was bent over, holding onto his knees, trying to catch his second wind. He and Tookie had just smacked a pole on 16th in Nash trying to get here. They'd both jumped out and ran. "Hold up." He threw up one finger. He said, "Me and Tookie—we—we jus—just took the police—on a high speed—high-speed chase. We was dirty so—but fuck that. I saw—Tip. She came out of the hospital. Told me to come—holla at you."

Then he collapsed on the floor, still out of breath. "She wanted me to tell you she signed them papers for 'em to go ahead and get those bullets out 'em."

We knew the doctors had said there was a chance Doe could die if they went in. There was a bullet close to his heart. There was also one at the base of his spine that could cause paralysis.

Smoke said, "She needs you, she was cryin' and shit."

I jumped up, Moo put his head down, praying for the best, and preparing for the worst.

"Moo, I'm comin' with you!" I said.

He looked at me and shook his head. "It's too dangerous, Hood," he said.

"Fuck that, I wanna—"

"What the fuck I just say, huh?" He jumped to his feet and walked up on me. We were nose-to-nose. He made sure of it. "Don't move! You hear me? Don't move!" He gave me his back then said, "Y'all don't let them leave until I get back!" He was out.

***

15 Minutes Earlier

Tip and Fry were asleep at Doe's bedside when they were suddenly awakened by the machine monitoring his heart. Doe's body started convulsing.

"Doe—Doooeee!" Uncle Fry yelled, attempting to hold his body still.

"Nurse! Nurrseee!" Tip screamed, pushing the red emergency button. The nurse rushed in. "Something's wrong! Oh, my God! Help 'em! What's wrong?" Tip yelled.

The nurse said, "He's having a seizure! Code blue! Doctor Mitchel!" she yelled.

The doctor ran in. "He's going into cardiac arrest! Prep him for surgery!" He looked at Tip. "You need to sign those papers, now! Ms. Phillups, there's a chance he'll live! But if you don't—" Then all sorts of white coats rushed in.

"I'll sign! I'll signnn, Doe—Doooeee!" she cried as they rushed his body out of the room and down the hallway.

"This is as far as you can go, I'm sorry."

"Wait!" Tip was trying to get past the doctor.

"Wait in the waiting room! We'll do everything we can! Go get those papers signed. Nurse, get her those forms!" he ordered as he rushed into the operating room.

K'ajji

Chapter 32

Doe

I could hear them, but for some reason, I could 't open my eyes. Tip and Uncle Fry were screaming my name. Now I heard different voices, male and female.

"*Wash! Gloves!*" *one voice yelled.*

"*Doctor, his vital signs are decreasing!*" *another said.*

"*Okay, let 's get him on the table.*"

"*Flatline, we 're losing him!*"

"*No, we 're not! Get me 4cc 's of epinephrine now! Get those X-rays up on the lightbox! This kid has a chance! Let 's do our best to save him!*" *He glanced at his chart.* "*Okay nurse, tell me what you see in those X-rays! Do we have a pulse?*"

"*Not yet, doctor!*"

"*Well, get the defibrillator, damn it!*"

"*Charging! Clear!*" *a female voice yelled.*

"*He has a projectile lodged near the pulmonary artery and another one in the vertebral column!*" *someone yelled.*

"*Get me a pulse! I need a pulse.*"

"*Cleearrr!*" *I heard the female voice yell again.*

Okay, now I can see them. I had to get past that light. But why am I on the ceiling? Hey! Heeeyyy, up here! Can y 'all hear me? What the fuck 's going on? Damn, that looks like me on that table. I know that ain 't my brotha, Mooo! Moo-Moo.

"*We 've got a pulse! But it 's light!*" *a nurse said.*

"*It 'll have to do!*"

I 'm thinking, what ah have to do?

"*Okay, he 's under,*" *the doctor told everybody around him.*

Hey, they cuttin' me open! Hold up! Aye! Ayee! Wait a minute! Waaaittt! Wait. Where this lady come from? She ain 't no doctor. She damn sure don 't look like one and she lookin' right at me. She lookin' real familiar. She got this glow behind her—I must be dreamin'.

"Domain! Domain! Don 't go, come back!" Her voice sounded choppy, like static in a radio frequency or some shit.
But—I know that—I know that voice, that face. "Mm—ma, is that you?"
   "Yes, son. Come back, Moozeere and Tasha need you!"
   "Ma, you can hear me? What's goin' on? What 's happening to me?"
   "Yeah, baby, I can hear you. Come down to me!"
   "Ma, I'm tryin', but I can 't move!"
   "You have to will yourself son! Close your eyes, use your heart and your mind. God please, he's not ready yet!" She turned, pleading to the light behind her. *"Give him another chance!"* She looked up at me and said, *"Talk to the Creator, son! Ask Him to let you come down. That I may walk you back!"* She stretched out her arms to me. "Okay, Maaa!" I agreed and closed my eyes.

Chapter 33

Moo

I walked into the hospital, not knowing what to expect. My niggas outside couldn't tell me anything. When I got to the waiting room, everybody was there, Trina, Mahalia, Yana, Auntie Iris, Uncle Fry, of course, Tip and a few more relatives and friends. Jahnahdah was out there in a wheelchair. China and Mona were right there by her side. The look in Tip's eyes damn near crushed me. Everybody was in tears. She ran to me and we embraced.

"What's wrong? What happened? What they say?" I whispered.

"They sa-sayyy—he go—got a fifty-fifty channnnce!" she cried.

"Be strong, don't you worry," I told her. That's when I looked up and saw her. She'd finally caught up with my ass. It was Gina, holding two cups of coffee.

She walked over to us. "Ms. Phillups, come on, here's your coffee ma'am. He gon' be alright. Let's sit you down, come on," she said, handing Tip her cup. She was eyeing me the entire time. Taking Tip by her arm, she sat her down, looking back over her shoulder and mouthing the words, "I need to talk to yo' ass!" She was mugging.

I'm thinking, *Damn, why niggaz ain't tell me she was up in here? Fuck she do? Sneak up in this bitch?* It didn't matter, I wasn't leaving. By the looks of it, neither was she.

"You gon' be a'ight?" she asked Tip. She nodded yes. "Y'all keep an eye on her. Excuse me for a sec, Ms. Phillups. I hope it's okay, I need to speak with Moozeere for a minute."

"Okay," Auntie replied, barely able to hold her head up.

Gina grabbed me by my hand like I was five and led me out of the room and down the hallway. I waited until we were clearly out of sight before I jerked my hand away from her.

"Fuck you doin' here, Gina?" I asked through clenched teeth.

"Moozeere, boy!" she said, pointing her finger at me. "You know damn well why I'm here! I told 'em to call me if anything changed in your brother's condition! I know it's—this is a bad time. But I just left another crime scene, not even an hour ago, and I think I already know the answers to all my questions. I think my problem is standin' right here in front of me."

I turned to try to walk away but she grabbed me, spun me around, and pushed me up against the wall.

"Moozeere, don't you turn yo' back on me! I know whatchu up to! Now I told you before, I'd hate to be the one to come get you — again! But if your name comes up in any of these murders, I'm gon' do my job! You understand me? I should take yo' ass in, right now cause I know you dirty. I know cause I see at least one gun print on yo' ass as we speak! But yo' brother in that operating room, right now and I know your family needs you. Just know I'm on to yo' ass. Now, gone, getcha ass in there, and console your auntie 'nem. They can't lose both of y'all."

"They ain't gon' lose neither one of us!" I threw my jacket back over my shoulders, adjusted my guns, and walked off. I looked back at her and she had her arms crossed, lips pressed to the side, shaking her head.

She said, "Tuh, keep thinkin' it's a game. Just know when yo' ass sleep, I'm workin'!"

I walked back and reentered the waiting room, but Gina soon followed. Now she had her ass over there whispering something to Jahnahdah. I wondered what she was saying. I hated how her punk-ass thinks she knows everybody. Anyway, the hours went by, we waited and waited. Soon, everybody had cried themselves to sleep except me and Gina. We just sat there in silence, staring at each other. It was 8:38 in the morning when the doctor finally walked in.

I tapped Tip, she started waking everybody up. "The doctor here y'all! Y'all get up!"

"How is he?" I asked. He saw the concern in my face.

I saw when it dawned on him I looked exactly like the patient he'd just operated on. He smiled. "He's a fighter," he said. "He's fast asleep but he'll live. We were able to successfully abstract both bullets. However, we won't know if the damage done to the vertebral canal caused paralysis until he's awake. We'll run a few tests. Hopefully, he'll be just fine."

"When will we be able to see 'em!" Jah yelled with a smile.

"Uh, soon, they'll be moving him shortly. He'll be on the recovery wing. He needs to rest. Right now, he's heavily sedated. I'd say, give him an hour or two give or take and you'll all be able to see him as well as talk to him. Alright, folks!" he said, cupping his hands together and smiling.

"Thank, God!" Tip yelled in excitement, hugging the doctor.

"Thank you, Jesus!" Mahalia praised right behind her.

"Okay, I'm outta here," Gina said. "I'm sure my face isn't one of the first he wants to see. But tell Domain I'll be back." She gave everybody hugs except me. She looked at me and rolled her eyes, saying, "Send him my love, Moozeere! And remember what I told you." Then she walked over to me, leaned in, and whispered, "And by the way, tell them lil' boyzzz you got outside, I see 'em. But do they see me? A'ight, Ms. Phillups, family, and friends!" However, as she was walking out she turned and said, "Oh, Jahnahdah, you remember anything, call me." Then she left.

Yana fucked around and asked where were the babies? At first, I was lost because I had no idea who the hell she was referring to. I had forgotten all about them.

I said, "Ohhh, th-they straight. Matter fact, let me call 'em, right now and give 'em the good news."

Auntie Iris could try to hide her daughter all she wanted to. Little did they know their Lil' girls were far from being babies now. Me, I was contemplating my next move — to touch those pussy-ass niggas!

K'ajji

Chapter 34

J. L.

He'd called a meeting on 39th in Burleigh. Everybody at the table was of great importance to The Zoo. J.L. circled the table in his all-black Versace suit and stopped behind his cousin.

"So, Burleigh Rick, what happened?" J. L. asked, standing behind him.

"I oughn't know, all I know is—"

"Fuck you mean you don't know! Muthafuckaz done got us for ten bricks and two-hundred and twenty-five gees and you don't know what happened?"

Burleigh Rick said, "I had left to get some chicken from Church's. Dope-fiend Eddie said all he saw was five niggaz dressed in hockey masks run—"

"Fuck that! All you got to tell me is what some dope-fiend-ass nigga said he saw! Huh?" J.L. yelled, wrapping a garrote around Burleigh Rick's neck and snatching him backward out of his chair.

Burleigh Rick reached for his neck but it was too late. He squealed like a wild hog. As he squirmed and kicked he broke one of the legs of the table, causing it to collapse at one end. The scuffle only lasted about a minute, blood gushed and squirted from Burleigh Rick's throat as J. L. twisted the homemade weapon he'd manufactured from barbwire and an old broomstick. Twisting, again and again, all the while staring at his team, he struck bone. Burleigh Rick finally stopped struggling, he was dead. He was also damn-near beheaded.

As he released his grasp, J. L. was out of breath and covered in blood. He'd gotten old and out of shape. It had been a while since he'd put in some work.

He kicked his cousin's obese frame and he said, "That was a million-dollar bucket of chicken you stupid muthafucka!" He was breathing heavily. "Now!" he said as he wiped his hands with a towel Po handed to him. "We've taken loss after loss these past few weeks. How y'all think the streets lookin' at that?" He looked around. "Ross, Po, get 'em outta my sight! I don't want 'em found. The rest of you take this as a lesson.

"Ain't no nigga exempt around this muthafucka! He was supposed to secure the package! We losing a war against some young street punks! I got money older than these niggaz! Here it is, I done buried Chaka and I had to send my other sister up outta here this mornin'!" He looked at Lil' Zoo. "We gon' ride for yo' momma and every nigga we done lost. This shit has gotten out of hand!

"We don't know for sure who's responsible for the shit that went down last night. Niggaz could see us as being weak cause we ain't took care of them twins yet. I can't blame 'em for tryin' us. Then again, 3C could be behind it. Tre, everything remains the same with you. How the spot over there lookin'?"

"Shit, we doin' numbers," Tre-Rida replied.

"What kind of numbers?"

"I'd say about thirty-thou a night. Teem ain't told you?"

J.L. said, "For, Fatima, to be my accountant, she sure get to actin' senile when it comes to mentioning my money she done collected."

Tre said, "Well, that's yo' bitch, nigga, not mine. Maybe she gettin' tired of playin' number two to old Cupcakes. Maybe she savin' some of that money for a rainy day." He smiled, rubbing his beard.

"Teem ain't stupid. She ain't goin' nowhere. Congo, I'm puttin' you in charge of all the spots Burleigh Rick ran. Anybody asks about 'em, y'all don't know nothin'. I'll deal with his momma 'nem. Tre—you, Lil' Trell, Church, and Brando gather up some more niggaz and go at 3C. I'm gon' try to find out what I can about what went down last night. Somebody find me this dope-fiend, Eddie. Anybody found out exactly who hit Geom and Class yet?"

Zoo said, "We all know it was 3C. Look, if niggaz ridin' I want in, Unk."

"Zoo, come on nephew, ya leg still broke. Plus, I don't want you out there like that," J.L. replied.

"Ain't nobody gon' ride for mine like me! Where yo' gun at Unk? When you gon' stop hidin' like you—"

"A'ight boy, you better watch yo' muthafuckin' tongue!"

"Or what, you gon' kill me like you just did cuz, huh? I ain't got time for this shit!" Zoo got up and grabbed his crutches. Then he said, "Me and mine up outta here!" He hobbled out the room, J.L. nodded as his crew followed.

Congo said, "You know he right, don't you?"

"Whatchu mean?" J.L. asked.

"You may have to dust off the old guns and come out of retirement. You playin' poltergeist ain't always been the best route."

J. L. said, "You know what, you might be right."

U-Tee, Zoo, Trell, and Proof rode four deep in Tee's '72 Chevy Impala. U-Tee was the oldest and tried to calm Lil' Zoo's mind as he drove.

"Just be cool, Zoo," he said. "You already know. We all ready to ride for Chaka 'nem."

"Fuck that nigga! Shit don't stop just cause he say so! Blue and Famo 'nem still in the hospital and this nigga tuckin' his tail like a bitch! He quick to give orders, though. My legs ain't got shit to do with my mufuckin' fingers! While this bitch hidin', it's us that's takin' all the slugs! Ain't you niggaz gettin' tired of goin' to funerals?"

"Hell yeah. I know I am," Proof said.

"Look how he just did Burleigh Rick!" Zoo said. "Talkin' 'bout a mil."

"That was outta order," Trell said, staring out the passenger side window.

Zoo said, "You muthafuckin' right! Without us, he wouldn't have been able to build none of this shit! You can't name one nigga that built an empire by himself."

Trell said, "I heard Geom momma and my auntie talkin' last night. Accordin' to them, they say J. L. stole some shit from some nigga name Teague back in the day. They think that's what all this bullshit about."

Zoo said, "You bullshittin'!"

"Dog, that's what my auntie told me. You know I hollered at her after Ms. Kayla left. She said J.L. used to Work for the nigga."

"Unk told us that the niggaz off 3C was tryin' to extort him out some money and that's why we at war."

"Nah man, I'm tellin' you. My auntie said my Uncle Spree was there. Them 3C niggaz came at J. L. at Sonny's; told 'em it was time to pay his dues. I guess the twins is the nigga Teague's sons or some shit. They originally from A.T.K. She said when them boy's pops got jammed up, J. L. was holdin' a lot of the man's product. She said your uncle kept all the man's shit and never looked back."

"Wait a minute, I know that name," Zoo said. He thought back, hearin' J. L. and Burleigh Rick talk about Teague when he was a shorty.

U-Tee knew this conversation was one they'd have to continue, but privately, as they pulled up to the spot on 34th. He said, "Hold on, it's too many niggaz out here. We'll holla
when we get in the house. It ain't that I don't trust our circle, I just think we should keep this amongst us until we come to a conclusion."

Brando, Fly, Church, and some more Zoo niggas were posted out in front of the spot.

"What up folk-and-nem?" Brando yelled, greeting each one of them. Everybody shook up, showing the lil' homies love.

Fly said, "What that nigga J.L. talkin' about? What up Zoo? You a'ight?"

"Yeah, I'm good," Zoo replied dryly. He was in deep thought.

U-Tee said, "Shit, we gotta handle some shit. I gotta holla at Zoo real quick. Who up in here?" he asked, walking up the steps.

"Nobody, go ahead," Brando said.

Zoo, Trell, U-Tee, and Proof walked into the spot.

Fly said, "Damn, y'all see that look in the nigga Zoo eyes? My nigga goin' through it about his momma. No bullshit."

Brando said, "Shit, what nigga wouldn't."

Once inside the spot, U'Tee locked all the doors and made sure all the windows were shut. He checked every room, they were alone.

He went back downstairs. "A'ight, we straight. Keep it low." They all took seats in the living room.

Zoo sighed and said, "So, Trell, you tellin' me all the nigga had to do was pay what he owed? And my momma and all ours a still be here?" There was a long pause.

Trell replied, "Exactly, my nigga."

"Damn," U-Tee said, rubbing his face in disbelief. Proof remained silent.

"Whatchu wanna do?" U-Tee questioned, looking at the hurt in Zoo's eyes.

He said, "We need to find dope-fiend Eddie."

***

Meanwhile, Moo, Tip, Fry, and Jahnahdah were at Doe's bedside. Although Jah was the first to see him, they were all taking turns getting in there. Nikki, Keba, and the rest of the family were still awaiting their turn. He hadn't been awake long, but Moo had let everybody holla at him. Now it was finally his turn to talk to his brother.

"How you feelin' lil' bro'?" he asked, gripping Doe's hand.

"They say I took five. What I tell you about that *lil* shit, nigga? I'ma big dog." They both smiled. "How long they talkin' about keepin' me?" Doe asked.

"I don't know. You'll have to ask the doctor or one of these nurses."

"Emma?" Doe questioned. Moo shook his head. Doe closed his eyes as his mind took him back to that night. Moo felt his grip strengthen. Doe said, "Bring it in close." He pulled Moo in, then leaned in within earshot, and said, "I saw momma." Moo couldn't believe his ears as he stared into his brother's eyes. "She brought me back, bruh. You wouldn't believe what she told me—"

They were interrupted by a tap on the door. "Excuse me," a nurse said as she entered the room. "You guys can still talk. I just need to run a few quick tests. Mr. Phillups, glad to see you're awake.

143

How do you feel?" she asked, shining a pen-light into both of his eyes.

"I'm a'ight," Doe replied.

She stepped to the end of the bed, removing the end of the blanket which covered his feet. Using gloved hands, she ran her index and middle fingers up his left foot than his right one. "Mr. Phillups, can you feel my fingers?" she asked. "You're a strong young man."

"Yeah, I feel 'em."

"You're wiggling your toes, that's good. Your motor skills seem to be fine. Can you move your legs for me?"

"Yup, see?" Doe raised his knees.

Jah said, "Yeah, everything works okay. I made sure!" Everybody laughed.

"Okay, then, excellent!" the nurse said with a smile, turning red in the face. "I'll be sure to inform the doctor you're doing great. Excuse me, you guys." She was trying to get out of there.

"Aye nurse! How long am I gon' be here?" Doe asked.

'I'm not sure," she said. "We'll have to ask the doctor, okay?"

"Oh, a'ight."

"If you need anything, just push the red button. I'll come running." She smiled.

Moo asked, "What she say, Doe?" thinking of his mother.

"We'll talk later. We gotta go see Teague, together."

"You see who popped you?"

"It was Po and from what Jah told me, and what she described, that was him, too. Moo, if they happen to discharge her before me—"

"Come on, bruh, I already know. But, believe me, she ain't goin' nowhere without you."

***

Tee

These my lil' niggaz. Shit, Zoo ain't wrong for feeling the way he feels. So, I'm rolling with them against all odds. We're keeping the plan amongst us. There's no need for everybody being in our business. I know for a fact that Congo's big gorilla-looking ass, Spree, Po, and Ross would die for the nigga J.L. the same way I'd die for mine. The only nigga that I think would get caught up with emotions, trying to decide who to roll with, would be Tre-Rida. We're all from the same deck but there's always that separation somehow.

You got niggas having money to niggas having more money. Then you got the killas and niggas who simply aren't that. You've also got stickup kids who kill for the thrill of it. You know, those niggas who just love the thrill of taking shit, including lives. Say, for instance, my nigga Proof, he's a fifteen-year-old animal! I grabbed him up and we hit the ground running, looking for this nigga, dope-fiend Eddie. For some reason, today was different than most. Somehow, he was nowhere to be found in the immediate area which was unlike him.

My worst fear was that somebody else had already snatched him up. We'd already hit all the spots he frequented the most, trying to score a quick buck to get that next blow. But we couldn't find him, Proof was growing impatient. It was early, the police were riding, and we had bangers.

"Damn, where the fuck this dirty, dope-fiend-ass nigga at?" Proof yelled, glancing at every yard and down every alley we passed.

"Just chill, lil' nigga. He could be anywhere. We just gon' keep ridin' and we gon' keep lookin'. He out here somewhere," I told him.

Suddenly, our luck changed for the better. When we pulled up to the light on 27th in Atkinson, Proof spotted a bunch of hypes to our left. They were standin' in front of some apartment buildings down on 28th.

"Turn left, nigga, look!" he said as he tapped my arm. "It's a bunch of them bloodsuckaz right down there! Damn, I think I see his ass!"

"I can't just bust a left, nigga! I ain't in the lane! We gon' come back around. He ain't goin' nowhere."

"Fuck that, I'm out, right here." Proof opened the car door and jumped out. "Just hit the block and park on Roosevelt. If he down there, I got 'em."

Before I could say anything, he was moving down the block like a shadow under the sun. I hit the block, dipped to the curb, and waited. I was checking my rearview and watching the block in front of me. Seconds later, I heard the thunderous sound of his regulator.

Boom! Boom! Boom!

Then I saw him running from in between one of the houses down the street in front of me. I pulled down on him in the stolen trap. I was riding beside him as he ran up the block.

"Get yo' ass in!" I yelled. "Come on, nigga! What the fuck!" He finally jumped in, out of breath. We sped off. "He dead?" I asked, glancing over at him.

"He—he ain't—if he can take three to the head, my nigga," he said and smiled.

"What about all the other fiends that was out there? Anybody, we know?"

"Hell nall! They got the fuck outta there as soon as I pulled the three minutes to four." I couldn't do anything but laugh at the lil' crazy nigga "You should've been there," he said.

"Them bitches scattered like roaches!"

Our first priority was taken care of. We couldn't have Eddie helping J.L. put shit together. We needed shit to stay indistinguishable if things were to go as planned. Whether the next move would go as smooth was something I couldn't determine, we had to get at 3C.

Chapter 35

Hood

It had been weeks and it was finally the day I'd been waiting on. Doe was coming home from the hospital and I'd finally get a chance to see him. Due to the ongoing drama, Tip's crib stayed surrounded by shooters. He wasn't going there. Moo came and picked me up and dropped me off at some strange crib out on Mill Road. He didn't even tell me whose crib it was. All I knew was the muthafucka was decked! You know as soon as he left my nosey ass was all through that bitch.

It didn't take me long to figure out the spot was his. The downstairs told me nothing. There were picture frames with no pictures. So, I went upstairs, a lone picture of our mother sat on his dresser in his bedroom. Stuck in the frame of the mirror of the dresser were pictures of all of us visiting Teague. In one of the dresser drawers, I found pictures of us from when we were little as hell, staying on Atkinson.

He had me showing all thirty-twos. Searching the closet, I recognized some of the clothing I'd seen him in. There was a safe in the back of that bitch. I wondered how much money he had in it, but it was locked. His ass still hadn't hit us off for that lick we hit. I had to make it my business to remind his ass when they got back. He had all kinds of guns mounted on the back of his bedroom door.

Something just told me to look behind that bitch! My eyes went straight to the top and lit up! I guess it was my newfound love for the foe-five. I took one of them off the door, leaving its twin hanging there. It was like—it was calling me! So, I grabbed her as well, I had to hold both of those pretty bitches! I had two new ones he'd given me, but these were different. I heard a noise downstairs. I put the guns back and rushed back towards the stairs.

"Hood! Tasha! Where yo' ass at?" I heard Moo yell.

Reaching the top of the steps, I yelled, "Here I come boy! Dang!"

"I know you ain't been up there ramblin' through my shit!" He was woofing but I paid him no mind.

"Doe-Dooooe!" I yelled, running to him with tears flowing.

"I'm here, sis, don't be cryin'." He hugged me tight.

"I'm—I'm jus—just so happy to see youuuu! Moo-Moo wouldn't—he wouldn' let me."

"I know, I know. Shhhhh, it was for the best. Look, look at me." He grabbed me by the shoulders, looking me in my eyes. "It was for the best. I know you wanted to be there. I would've wanted the same thing. Come on, let's sit you down." He took me by my hand and we sat on the couch.

I dried my tears, looking at Moo sitting on the loveseat. "Doe, Moo ain't gave us our share of that money! I seen that safe upstairs!"

"What money?" Moo said.

"Boy, stop playin' with me! You know goddamn well what money!"

Doe said, "Oh, I heard about that. Y'all handled y'all business. Bruh, why you ain't hit 'em off yet?"

"Shit!" Moo said, waving me off. "I was just holdin' it fo' 'em, that's all. What they lil' asses gon' do with it anyway?"

"It don't matter!" I said. "That's—"

"Chill! Chill!" he said. "I got you." He got up and headed toward the steps.

I said, "You should let me get them two .45s on your door, too!" He ain't say shit. He just looked back and smiled. Looking at Doe, he looked different. I said, "You lost some weight, bruh. You hungry? Let me fix you somethin' to eat. Moo got plenty shit up in here." I walked towards the kitchen and he picked up the remote, turning on the T.V.

Doe yelled, "Hell yeah! I could use a real breakfast! Hook me up!"

"I got you!" I yelled back, grabbing the milk, eggs, and cheese out the fridge. "Pancakes, eggs, sausages and hash browns, comin' right up!" I knew his favorites.

"Thank you, sis!" he yelled from the living room.

Moo came back downstairs with a leather briefcase. He sat it on the island in the kitchen. "That's fifty thou in there," he said. "I even put ten in there for Bri and Lue and they wasn't even there. I still gotta hit Lesis and Yetta, too. I ain't forgot about y'all."

"That's fifty thou!" I exclaimed I'd never held nor had a thousand at one time.

"Yeah, make enough of that shit for all three of us. I'm hungry, too," he said with a smile. "I told you I had you." He smiled again and walked out of the kitchen.

I walked over and opened the case. The two .45s I'd asked for were sitting on top of all that money. I remember thinking, *My bitches ain't gon' believe this shit! We ri-iiich.*"

K'ajji

Chapter 36

Moo

When Doe told me about seeing momma, I really didn't know how to take it. Was this just some dream he'd had subconsciously, or was it real? I mean, him dying and seeing mom in this translucent white dress, standing next to the doctors as they fought for his life, them walking hand-in-hand down Atkinson to the old house on 10th. Then what she told him had me fucked all the way up.

Doe said when they got to the crib, she told him she had to show him something. They walked up on the porch and she opened the door. They walked inside and she told him to look. He said he saw us asleep in front of the TV on the living room floor. Mom was sitting at the dining room table talking to John Le Von. They were drinking Crown Royal and playing tonk.

As he puffed a joint he asked her if she 'd go get him some more ice. She smiled, took his glass, and headed to the kitchen. Quickly, he pulled a bottle of Visine from his pocket, spiking her drink with its content. He tried to cuff' it when she came back into the room, but she 'd noticed his sudden movement.

"What's that?" she asked.

He showed her the bottle, it was damn near empty. "Aw, nothin' a lil' Visine," he said. smiling. "I ain't supposed to be drinkin' or smokin' Cuppy gon' act a damn fool."

He laughed, squirting some in his eyes then sliding it back into his pocket.

She said, "Cuppy need to kick that ass if you doin' shit behind her back." As she sat down he reached for her thigh, but she smacked his hand. "Business, nothing personal," she said. "Do she know you here? I know people seein' yo' car and I don't need—" she said, pointing her finger at him.

"I apologize," he said, raising his hands. "Forgive me. Yeah, she knows where I'm at. I told her Teague sent word through you about some business that needs to be taken care of."

"Okay cause if it's gon' be a problem, you need to go."

"Nah, nah now. No problem, she knows I 'm here. We can have a few more drinks then I 'm gone. I 'll bring you that money and that horse in the mornin'. We gon' get 'em out."

"I 'll drink to that!" My mom raised her glass. He went to give her a toast, but she pulled her glass back. She said, "Two million, right?"

"Yeaaahhh!" he said. "Two mil." They clanked their glasses together and both drank up.

He quickly poured her another. They laughed, talked, and sipped quietly, careful not to disturb the sleeping children. Within 15 minutes, my momma passed out. That's when he pulled off the belt he was wearing and tied it around her arm. He injected her with the hotshot, collected the glasses, the cards and wiped the table down in an attempt to rid any evidence of him being there. He saw Tasha stir and turnover in her sleep.

He pulled his gun, walked over to where we were, and stood over us as we slept. Doe said once he saw we were still asleep, he uncocked the .44 and slid out the door. As my mother's body reacted to the drug her body shook and she rolled out the chair and onto the floor. He said as he watched all this unfold, he fell to his knees screaming for us to wake up, but we didn't. My mother's spirit touched his shoulder. He looked up at her, she smiled and said, "It is okay Domain. I 'm alright, I'm at peace. But Teague, Tasha, and Moozeere need to know I would never leave them. When you awake to assure yourself that this was no dream, go see Teague. He 'll verify that he told me three weeks before I passed to talk to John and retrieve what belonged to him. Tell Teague I said I love him and to please forgive me. Now, go up to your room. When you open the door, you 'll awake. I love you, son. You've been given a second chance. Go!" She disappeared.

Doe walked up the steps, opened our bedroom door, and woke up in the hospital to Jahnahdah standing at his bedside, smiling.

Chapter 37

Teague

"2-5-0-2-4-4! Phillups! You have a visit, 2-5-0-2-4-4! Phillups, you have a visit! Report to the rec fence!" the officer working the cage at outside rec yelled over the loudspeaker.

"Teague, that's you, big homie," Spade said.

"I know. I hear 'em," he said, still holding the weights in the air.

"Come on then—breathe—and push 'em out! Last two. One!"

"Ahhhhh!" Teague yelled.

"Two, good set. Drop 'em on the rack," Spade coached Teague on the bench as he pressed out his last rep of ten at 365 pounds. Teague sat up, drenched in sweat. "You good?" Spade asked him because it looked as if he was in deep thought about something.

"Yeah, I'm good." Teague stood up.

"You expectin' somebody?" Billion asked, handing him his shirt.

"Nah, not today. But they here now, whoever it may be, young dog."

Lil' Man said, "I hope it's a good one. It could be yo' lawyer."

"Yeah, let me go jump in this water real quick. I'll holla at you niggaz later." Teague shook-up with each of them.

When he got to Young Zero, he held the shake firm. He said, "Walk with me."

"What up on 10th?" Zero asked as they walked towards the gate.

"Grab one of them shivs from Goon and meet me by the showers. I need you on *S* for a few minutes, lil' homie."

"A'ight, I'm there." Zero turned back to cuff the sword.

Teague went to his cell, he grabbed his clothing, his shower shoes, and his mesh bag and headed for the showers. When he got there, Zero was posted as promised. He was in and out within seven minutes tops. When he made it to the visiting room and they buzzed him in, he didn't recognize any familiar faces as he walked through. He stopped at the desk to drop off his visitor's slip and asked the officer where he was seated. The officer told him it was at table 57 in the vending area. He walked into the area where the machines were — and there were his boys.

"Aaayyyeee, Doe!" He grabbed him and hugged him.

"Son, I thought we'd lost you for a minute. Let me look at you! You losin' weight?"

"Yeah, pops, I lost a few. That's the same thing Hood asked. This what five slugs do to a nigga!" Doe smiled with his arms spread wide.

"Bitch ass nigga done shot my boy. When you get out of the hospital?" he asked, giving Moo a hug.

"I got out today. We had to come see you right away. It's important."

"Anytime is good for me. Moo-Moo, what's on your mind? You know I can tell when somethin' bothering y'all. Talk to me."

Moo said, "We'll holla, let's have a seat. Whatchu want out the machines?"

Teague replied, "Shit, grab us some of everything, burgers, chicken, fries, pizza, chips—the works."

"What kind of pop you want?" Moo asked.

"Mountain Dew. Doe, what's going on, how you feel?" he asked when Moo left to go get the food.

"I'm alive and ready to murda—"

"Whoa, hold that down son," Teague whispered. "Don't forget where we at. J. L. still breathin', huh?" Doe nodded. "Moo ain't got 'em yet? I hear it was the nigga, Po, that shot you. He ain't dead yet, either?"

"Nall, them niggaz ain't been seen. Pops, I—I got somethin' to ask you. I really don't know how to say it."

"What, what is it, son?" Moo came back to the table.

"A'ight, this shitz hot! What I miss? You ain't ask him yet, did you?" Moo asked, setting everything down and taking a seat.

"Nall, not yet." Doe dropped his head.

"Ask me what? Will y'all tell me what the fuckz goin' on?" Teague looked back and forth between them.

Doe just said it, "I saw momma."

"What—whatchu mean you saw yo' momma?" Teague reached for a burger and unwrapped it.

Doe said, "When I was in the OR I died, and she came and got me."

Teague paused, setting the burger down. First, he sniffled and then sighed, rubbing his eyes, his brain was trying to take in what was being said to him. His eyes veered towards Moo. The look in his eyes told him Doe was serious.

Moo said, "I know, I was thinkin' the same thing. But just listen."

Doe said, "Did you tell—" he was nervous. "Did you ask momma to get somethin' from the nigga John LeVon a few weeks before she passed?"

Teague was dumbfounded, he said, "Three weeks—how—how y'all know about that? John—"

"Momma told me!" Doe cut him off. "She came to me and took me back to the house. She—she showed me everything that happened that night, pops."

Teague said, "So—so you sayin'—"

"J.L. killed momma," Moo said. "She ain't overdose. That nigga killed her!"

Doe said, "She was supposed to get two million and some bricks, right?" Tears began to stream down Teague's face. Out of all the years they had come to see him, they'd never seen him shed a single tear, until now. "She told me to tell you she loves you and ask that you please forgive her."

Teague said, "Intimate, my—my baby died, tryin' to look out for me. Listen—don't kill J. L. Just kill everything around him. I know it's a lot to ask. I'm coming home, I want that nigga for myself." He looked both of them in the eyes.

Moo said, "You comin' home, pops?"

"Yeah," he said. "This Jew, Henak, is a beast! Doe tell me everything yo' momma told you, verbatim, from beginning to end.

K'ajji

Chapter 38

Hood

We were higher than a mountain lion. It was our first time calling ourselves smoking weed. It was Friday night and Bri's momma was pulling a double. We were all over there chilling, watching *A Nightmare on Elm Street,* and eating pizza. Auntie Yana even let Lue come out that night to attend the sleepover.

"Bitch, I'm tellin' you, fuck that! Shit, Hood, you the one on the phone with the nigga every night! And for what? Nigga gon' give us $10,000 apiece! You know damn well we got at least a quarter mil outta that house!"

"Um-hmm, and that's just the money," Sweets said, adding her two cents.

She and Mula's thirsty asses were trying to convince the rest of us to hit Tre-Rida and the others without Moo, Doe, or any help from 3C, period. I was trying to explain to them that we hadn't spent hardly any of the money we had. But they weren't trying to hear shit.

"I don't know y'all," I said.

"Bitch, you see how easily we got in and out that muthafucka last time?" Mula said.

"Yeah, we did that, huh?" I said, taking a bite of my slice of pizza.

"You, damn right!" she said.

Sweets said, "So, call that nigga and tell 'em you wanna kick it."

"When, tonight?" I questioned around a mouth full of cheese and sausage.

Lue said, "Ugh, Hood! Chew your food, swallow then talk! Don"t nobody wanna see all that!" Her lil' face was all scrunched up.

I said, "Y'all think he'll kiss me like this? Aaaah!" I showed them a mouth full of chewed up food, fucking with them. Everybody laughed.

Bri said, "Hold up! Quiet! Quiet!" We all paused. "Let me answer that. Hell—h-e-l-l—nall!"

We all burst out laughing. My ass almost choked on that pizza, but I swallowed it.

I said, "For real, though! How we gon' do the shit? We ain't got no masks, no nothin'."

"Now it sounds like you tryin' to make excuses, hoe," Mula said. "Fuck we got all these gunz for if we ain't gon' use 'em? I know you ain't scared?"

"What, scared? You acting like—fuck it. Let's vote on this shit. By a show of hands who think—" Sweets and Mula's hands shot to the ceiling, smiling and shit.

"Damn, y'all scandalous ass hoes ain't give a bitch a chance to ask the damn question, did y'all? Who?" I rolled my eyes.

"Well, spit it out, bitch!" Sweets said.

"A'ight, who think we should hit these niggaz? These two bitches workin' my nerves. Y'all fuckin' with my high."

When Lue and Bri raised their hands, I was shocked! They raised them shitz with the quickness, too.

I said, "Aw, a'ight then. Y'all serious!" I picked up the phone. "Y'all asses better come up with some gear and some masks," I said, dialing Tre-Rida's number.

Looking at the TV, Mula fired up another joint. "Don't even trip, I already got an idea," she said, holding her smoke and talking in a strained voice.

Lue said, "Ooh, what is it?"

Mula blew her smoke into the air and said, "Whatever you do, don't fall asleep." They all giggled.

The phone was still ringing, I said, "Ah, he-he hell! Y'all ke-keein' and shit! Roll up another one! Hello? This Tre? Whatchu doin'?" I shushed my girls. "Oh, you doin' me, huh? Yeah. You can come get me."

***

"Shoot, nigga! Shoot! Don't get scared now!" Spree yelled, standing over Tre-Rida as he crouched down with one knee on the floor.

"Damn, y'all loud. Who is that?" Hood asked, being nosey.

Tre said, "Aw, nobody, I'm over here breakin' shit. Bet I tenta-foe for two more then, nigga!"

"Bet, nigga!" Spree dropped two more geez.

"Ben!" Tre rolled the dice, hitting a nine. "Three hoes and me!" He rolled a six. "Up- jump ten!" he shouted as he rolled his point.

"Hello!"

"What up? You ready to give me some of that pussy or what?" Tre asked her, shaking the dice and holding the phone to his ear with his shoulder. He dropped another thousand and bet every nigga in the room. "Bet ta you, you, you, and you! What up!"

"Boy, that's all you tryin' to do is fuck? That's all you talk about. Yo' dick probably little as hell." She was trying to give him attitude. The P.Y.T.'s giggled quietly in the background.

"All you gotta do is try me. Nine! I'll bust that lil' oochie-coochie wide open. Nine, bitches!" He'd hit another point, standing there shaking the dice.

"Nigga, is you gon' roll them muthafuckaz or what?" Congo roared.

He was trying to win some of his money back. He, Tre, Kane, and Ross were at the spot gambling and he was down $10,000. Tre was striking their asses! He bet the room again.

"Tre-foe bitches!" He rolled, hitting another seven, picking $4,000. He stood up, scooping up all his winnings, and said, "Tasha, hold on for a minute." He stuffed his money everywhere and anywhere it would fit.

Congo said, "What up, nigga? I know you ain't runnin' off with my money?"

Tre smiled. "Yo' money lookin' a whole lot like my money in my pockets, right now, G. Personally, I ain't runnin' nowhere. But I am about to go pick this lil' pussy up real quick." Tre grinned at them. "I'll be back, though."

"Nigga, you on bullshit," Spree said.

Congo said, "Fuck 'em! I need a fader, not a friend. Shoot a thousand, bet a thousand! Anyone of you niggaz!"

Ross pulled out another wad. Tre picked the phone back up. "Aw, shit. Hello?" he said as he walked into the kitchen, opening the fridge.

Hood said, "Yeah, took yo' ass long enough."

"My bad, I had to take care of somethin' real quick. What up? Can I come get you or what?" He grabbed a juice and slammed the door.

"Yeah, I told you to come on. You ain't getting none, though so don't even try it."

He could tell she was smiling through the phone.

"That's what they all say. Where you at? You never told me where you live?"

"My momma told me to never tell," she teased.

"Oh, is that right?"

"Yup!"

"So, where can I come get you from?"

"How long you gon' be?" she asked.

"Shit, no longer than fifteen or twenty minutes. I gotta stop by the crib right fast and drop some of this money off. Then I'm on my way."

"You can pick me up at the corner of 45th in Townsend."

He said, "It's what—11:45 at night? And you about to be on the corner of 45th in Townsend? You ain't scared? Don't have me come all the way over there and you ain't gon' be out there."

"Boy, I'm from the hood. Don't too much scare me. I ain't none of them prissy bitches you used to dealin' with."

"A'ight then, fifteen minutes."

"A'ight, see you then. Bye." She hung up the phone. She said, "I can't believe I let you hoes talk me into this shit."

***

Fifteen Minutes Later

Tre pulled up on 45th in Townsend to see Hood and Mula standing on the corner. Hood opened the passenger side door but Mula stepped in front of her and leaned in.

She said, "Anything happens to my sis' I'm fuckin' you up, nigga!" She was smiling and at the same time, but she was dead serious.

Hood jumped in and they pulled off, speeding down Townsend to Fondulac. Then they hit Walnut.

"Where in the hell is you takin' me?" Hood asked as she reclined in the leather seat of the 'Vette.

"We ridin'," he said as he made a right onto 6th. When he did that, she knew he was taking her to a hotel.

She thought to herself, *This nigga done pulled up at the mutha-fuckin' Flitz!* Sucking her teeth she said, "Dang, why you have to bring me here? I told you that you wasn't getting none." He parked and turned off the engine.

"Pssst," he hissed. "Just come on." He jumped out of the car. He knew his mere presence had her pussy wet.

There weren't many who could resist him, in his own mind. She grabbed her purse containing the .45 and jumped out behind him.

"Damn, you ain't even attempt to feed a bitch or nothin'. Just pullin' up at the telly! You's a cocky ass nigga, huh?"

He smiled and said, "Cocky it is." He grabbed his piece and slid his keycard at the rear entrance, they walked in.

Ten minutes after they'd gotten into the room, he had Hood butt-ass naked, with her legs in the air as he tried to suck her skeleton out of her skin through her vaginal canal.

"Awwww, Shit! Whatchu—what chu—doinnn'! Ooooh!" she moaned.

Tre knew he had him one when he tried to slide two fingers into her. She could barely handle the tip of his thumb. Hood was still a virgin. He sucked that pussy for more than an hour, trying to get her loose. But no matter what he did, his attempts to put swipe in her failed. Wasn't nothing happening, and he was salty. But he couldn't really be mad at her. She'd let him try, though he was pissed.

His hormones were getting the best of him, so he continued to suck and lick. Then all of a sudden, he just jumped up. His mind was back on his money. He felt he was wasting time.

"Damn, this ain't gon' work. Put your clothes back on. I'm straight."

"Wha—what, why you stop?" Hood asked, still caught up in the heat of passion. She'd never had her pussy eaten before.

"Cause yo' shit too tight. I can't do nothin' with that. You ain't never been fucked before, have you?"

She just laid there, embarrassed. "Whatchu, mad?" she asked.

"Nah, I ain't mad at you. Put your clothes on, though. We leavin'."

"What, where we goin'?"

"I need to get back to this money. Get dressed, you can roll with me." He was thinking to himself, *I bet them niggaz still shootin' dice.*

***

When we left there, the nigga Tre made two major mistakes. The first was stopping where he laid his head with a bitch like me. The second, he took me to the spot. Niggaz had over a hundred thousand in a punk-ass dice game. Yeah, we had to touch these niggas. After all, I'd let him touch me.

Who said, *"Fair exchange ain't no robbery?"* I sure as hell didn't!

Chapter 39

Zoo

The murder of dope fiend Eddie had J. L. on the edge which was right where I wanted him. He felt there was a snake in the circle because nobody off Zoo was taking credit for the assassination. So, now he figured if it wasn't 3C, it was one of us who hit the spot. He was stuck in-between scenarios. There had only been a few selected niggas at that table when he announced that he wanted Eddie brought to him. Now, he didn't know who he could trust. Since his bullheaded ass wasn't trying to hear what the homie, U-Tee, was pulling his coat to, I went to holla at him myself.

We were at his favorite duck-off, his crib out by the airport. This nigga was so fucking full of himself we couldn't just talk in the living room, he had to invite me into his *den*. He sat behind his desk in this big dumb-ass black leather chair and threw his feet on top of it.

"What's on yo' mind, nephew?" he asked, puffing his Cuban cigar and blowing the smoke into the air.

I coughed and waved that shit out of my face. "I need you to tell these niggaz to fall back," I replied, still waving at that stanking-ass cigar smoke.

"Whatchu mean, fall back?" He was acting arrogant and it pissed me the fuck off. He knew muthafuckin' well Tee had just talked to him the day before about this shit.

"You see, ain't nobody doin' shit! They found my niggaz shot up in a muthafuckin' alley! And before we could bury 'em, niggaz come shoot up the visual! That's just the latest shit!"

Showing no emotion, he seemed to be looking past me and out the window. "Yeah, I heard they popped one of the lil' niggaz's momma and a few more people. The eulogy was sad. I wasn't able to attend, but I hear ain't nobody wanna go to the funeral after what went down out there."

"Unk, look, I'm tired of you sendin' yo' so-called killaz at niggaz and all mine takin' the hits! Ain't no cast on my leg no more! I don't wanna hear none of your excuses! I'm ridin' with or without your permission! Let us handle them niggaz!" I didn't even mention my momma's name because if I did, I felt I wouldn't have been able to hide my anger towards him. I knew how I wanted to end this nigga. I wanted him to mention her. Or see if he even had the balls to do so.

"I tell you what," he said, puffing his cigar. "A'ight, Zoo, I'll tell every nigga I got out there to hold tight. It's been weeks and ain't nobody I wanna see dead been fucked over. So, you right, I'll give you the chance to avenge ya momma. You lil' niggaz make it happen. I want them twins in front of me dead or alive."

That was all I needed to hear. I left that muthafucka with a smile on my face, although the past few months had been hell. Shit was about to change. See, it turns out my girl Goodie is a cousin of Chanel from A.B.'s lil' crew. I was eavesdropping on one of their phone conversations two days ago and I guess the nigga Moo-Moo's name must have come up. Goodie was blind to the game, she had no idea who was who in this war. I listened from the doorway of the bedroom as she laid across the bed on her stomach with her feet up, gossiping.

"Girrlll, you talkin' about the twin, Moo-Moo? Uh-huh, yup, they fine to be that dark. You know I prefer a light-skinned nigga. That's right, Zoo's bitch. Ain't they off 10th? I heard they be on Chambers now. Whaattt, he been tryin' to holla at A.B.? You tellin' me she ain't tryin' to see that nigga? Is she crazy? That nigga got money! Yup. at C.C.'s, and from what I heard he got some good ass—"

"Some good ass what?" I asked her, walking into the room where she could see me.

"Oh, hey bae. Chanel, let me call you back. Zoo just walked in. Yeah, um-hmm, bitch, I'm a go with you! A'ight, bye." She hung up the phone. She rolled over, jumped up, and hugged me, kissing me on my lips. Mmmuah!

"Mmm, what was that for? Who was that on the phone?" I asked her, staring into her eyes.

"Boy, that was my cousin Chanel. You know—Nell! She was just tellin' me about this party somebody havin' this weekend."

"Oh, yeah. Who?"

"Some niggaz, you probably don't even know 'em. You know Moo-Moo and Doe-Doe?" she asked.

"Do you?"

"Nah, but they names be ringin' when I be down at the shop gettin' my hair done. Why?"

"I need to holla at them niggaz. Street shit, that's all."

"Well, cuz say Moo-Moo be tryin' to holla at Any Bitch. I can try to get in contact with her and have her holla for you."

"You talkin' about Angie off Vienna, right?" I played dumb.

"Yeah. How you know her?"

"It's nothin'. Look, call yo' cousin back, tell her to call Angie and for them to come over here right now. Don't say shit else. I ain't here. You just tryin' to kick it."

"Why, what's up, bae?"

"Just do it."

***

2 Days Later

A.B., Trina, Chanel, Taliah, Ava, and Goodie walked into the club. C.C. Havannah's was packed wall-to-wall as they struggled to get through the crowd. Beautiful women were everywhere and niggas came dressed to impress. Although they were in the midst of war, the twins decided to throw a party. It was a clear indication they weren't worried about shit. If niggas had the balls to bring it, they were more than ready to ride. Goodie spotted the twins from amongst the crowd and pointed them out.

"A.B., there go the twins right there! You gon' go holla at "em?" she yelled over the loud music.

"Yeah, let me go over there. I'll catch up with y'all in a minute."

Ava said, "In a minute then, bitch! We about to get our drink on and dance with some of these fine-ass muthafuckaz up in here!"

"Shit, sure as hell is," Lil' Trina said, snapping her fingers to the sounds of *The Commodores*. She moved her body seductively as she sang along with the words, "She's a brick—hooouseee!"

A.B. walked over to the V.I.P. section where the twins, Jahnahdah and her crew, and some more of the 3C members were seated. *Stevie Wonder's Living For The City* blazed the speakers. As always, A.B. looked stunning, thick with caramel skin, just beautiful. She was wearing a white sequined dress and blazer. Her hair was swept up into a chignon with a side sweep of hair. She wore her red *fuck-me* pumps on her feet. She stepped to the table.

"Hey Moo, Doe, ladies, and fellas. May I take a seat?"

"Hell yeah, right here," Moo said, patting the leather beside him in the booth. "This is reserved just for you." He took her hand, pulling her toward him. She sat down. "You lookin' beautiful as ever tonight. I knew I invited you for a reason. How you doin', baby?"

"I'm doin' fine. And you?"

"Better now that you're here. Whatchu drinkin'?"

"Cranberry and pineapple, I don't wanna drink tonight. I gotta work in the morning."

"Cranberry and pineapple it is." He raised his hand, summoning the waitress to come take their order. "Anyway, what up? You know I been tryin' to get at you. Yo' momma been hatin' on me, huh?" He laughed, putting his arm around her. "I know she out to get me."

"She is not! She be tellin' me you be callin'. She ain't a fan of yours, that's for sure. She calls you the drug dealin' murderer." She laughed.

"Oh, is that why you been duckin' my calls? You believe that?"

"Nah, I just been busy with school and work. That's all."

"Oh, really?" He turned his lips to the side.

"Yeah, and why you so interested anyway? I mean with all these girlz up in here. I know half of 'em here to see you. I see 'em starin' when they walk through. You see 'em choosin'." She smiled.

"Come on, you killin' me here. You know why a nigga want you. You ain't just any bitch. I mean, not callin' you a bitch or nothin' but, I think you already know that. I understand yo' lil' slogan and shit, it's true. However, a mufucka wanna take it. Ain't nobody here like you. Not that I've met anyway."

"Awww, that's so sweet, but that nigga wouldn't like dat," she replied, rubbing the side of his face.

"Who, Boomer's broke-ass?"

"Never mind him, I got something to tell you but it ain't for everybody to hear. Come here, let me whisper it in your ear." She kissed his earlobe then whispered softly inside.

He was shocked by what he heard. All he could say was, "Aw yeah? When, tonight? Tryin' to see me? A'ight sounds good to me. I'll give you the address before we leave." He smiled, looking over at Doe. He said, "Bruh, we gon' be leavin' this bitch earlier than we intended tonight!"

Jahnahdah turned up her nose.

K'ajji

Chapter 40

Doe

The party was stupid dope. It was what came afterward which was hard for me to believe. Moo pulled me to the side and told me J.L.'s nephew wanted to holla at us. About what? His guess was as good as mine. But, if the nigga wanted to walk next to death, and see if he could conquer it, it was fine by me. Moo said he was talking about coming alone, unarmed, and to any location we wished. His fate rested in our hands. Of course, when I told Jah I had to leave to take care of some business, she threw a fit. Ever since I got blasted, she hated letting me out of her sight. We were at her new condo I'd copped for her on the outskirts of the city.

"Baby, I'll be back, I promise. I'ma have fifty niggaz and over a hundred gunz with me. No need to worry." I dried her tears. "Nahdah, just give me an hour, a'ight?"

"Okaaaay," she reluctantly replied, hugging my neck as tight as she could.

"Nahdah, you are never alone. I got people posted. Hear me? Honesty and Telesis gon' be outside until I get back." I kissed her and stared into her eyes once more just in case I didn't make it back.

Moo, Jilla, Thirty, and Tank were outside in the truck waiting on me. I jumped into the back and we pulled off. We had Zoo coming to one of the spots on 10th in Brown. We had that bitch armed up, the entire block! If Zoo tried anything stupid, there would be no way to survive. Come to think of it, he could very well be on a suicide mission. Although we didn't personally kill his momma, we did let Wintress and Yetta crazy asses loose on her. All was quiet when we pulled up to the spot. First, headlights flashed throughout the block and then houses on both sides up and down the street. Everything was in play. It was 4:15 a.m., he had 15 minutes. We walked into the spot to see niggas at every window with that heavy shit, them dragons! At 4:30 Zoo pulled up in front of the spot as scheduled.

***

Zoo

I pulled up on 10th in Brown at the address A.B. gave me to meet with Moo and Doe. As soon as I pulled over and parked, niggas in all black wearing ski masks surrounded the car with assault rifles.

"Getcha muthafuckin' hands up, nigga!" one yelled.

As I complied another one opened my door and snatched me out. He threw me on the ground.

"You bet not move!" I felt a barrel against the back of my head and another one in the middle of my back. "Frisk 'em! Make sure you pat 'em down good!" I was being searched, and thoroughly.

This move was one my niggas didn't agree with me on. But I assured them it was the only way.

"Turn yo' ass over!" I turned over and was frisked again at gunpoint.

"He ain't got nothin' on 'em?" one of the masked men asked.

"Nah, he good." The one who seemed to be in charge reached inside my car and blew the horn once.

Moo and Doe came outside, they stood me up.

Doe said, "Well, well, well, I thought you was bullshittin'. Either you gotta be the stupidest nigga God ever made, or you got a death wish. You lucky to be alive. Didn't we just light yo' ass up a few weeks ago? And you show up here?"

I said, "Didn't we just light yo' ass up a few weeks ago? You here, ain't you?" I was being sarcastic.

It wasn't a good idea. Now I had even more muzzles pointing in my direction. An AR-15 had my head leaning.

"Waaaittt, I don't want no smoke! I came to make y'all an offer! One that I feel you won't refuse. Jus—just tell 'em to be cool!"

Moo said, "Yeah, what's that?"

"Can we talk? Damn, I mean—" I motioned, emphasizing all the weapons pointing at me. Mainly the AR pressed against the side of my head.

Doe said, "Bring his ass in!" As I walked past them on the porch, he said, "You's a dead nigga if this is a waste of time. You know that, don't you?"

I just looked at them as some big burly nigga and four other niggas led me inside. They sat me down at the kitchen table. Everybody left the kitchen except the twins.

"Talk nigga!" Doe said, taking a seat across from me while Moo posted up, leaning against the counter.

I said, "Listen, I've lost a lot, my momma, my niggaz. I damn near lost my life. But I can't blame y'all. I solely blame my uncle. See, I never knew about the bullshit he'd pulled on y'all father. He told us that y'all was tryin' to extort him outta some money. I recently found out the truth behind all this. I'm willin' to make a deal with y'all where we can all come out on top. No more bloodshed in the streets."

"Whatchu got that you can offer us, lil' nigga?" Moo laughed.

"Unk got a hit out on y'all—dead or alive. I'll not only get y'all this nigga, I'll get y'all the merch he owes, and we can end this war."

"How you gon' do that?"

"Getting' him to y'all will be the easy part. He said he want y'all dead or alive. I'm just servin' up the alive part. Gettin' y'all what's rightfully yours won't be a problem either. He ain't got no more family in the game. After he's dead, I'll be runnin' Burleigh Zoo. He gave me and mine the green light to ride on y'all. As sure as I'm here, I give y'all my word—no more bullets a be headin' y'all direction from my way. I just need y'all to play y'all part. Don't kill no more of my niggaz. And in the next week or two, I'll serve this nigga up and get y'all the product."

Moo said, "Doe, you think we can trust this nigga?" He gave me the screwface.

"I wouldn't say trust. Let me ask you this. Why you ain't just kill 'em yo' self?"

"I could've," I said. "But that would be too easy. Why would I give him the pleasure of dyin' quickly by the hands of a loved one? I want him dead by means of his enemy. I wouldn't be sittin' here, right now if I wasn't serious about this shit. Y'all know it, I'm tryin' to see shit through!"

Doe got up and grabbed a piece of paper and a pen. He said, "We gon' take you up on your offer. Call this number when you got shit lined up. We'll give you a location on where to bring him."

"So, we got a deal?" I asked.

"Deal." Doe extended his hand, and so did Moo.

Chapter 41

Hood

Sunday -12:52 a.m.

I just talked to him, so I know he's in there. Tonight is the night and here we are, posted outside the spot Tre-Rida ran on 32nd in Burleigh, masked up like Freddy Krueger. Business looked slow and on my signal, we were going in. I looked to my left at Sweets and Mula, then to my right at Lue and Bri. I took a deep breath then exhaled. There was no turning back now. Holding up the .45s it was on and poppin'. We rushed the porch.

Booommm!

Sweets blasted the locks with the shotty and I kicked the door in.

Using my best impression of Moo, I entered, demanding respect! "Lay the fuck down niggazzz! Y'all know what-it-izzz!" My team fell in behind me, guns up!

One of the niggas yelled, "Oh, shit!"

There were four men and one tried to run into one of the bedrooms. We couldn't have that!

"Where you goin', bitch?" I said. "Lay down!"

Boom! Boom! Boom! I hit him in his back with three rounds. Tre showed no signs of fear, though the other two were screaming like bitches.

"Treeelll! Aww, my niggaaa! Nawww!" one screamed.

The robbery had turned fatal in seconds. There was no time for bullshit, I was on business. "Who else up in this muthafucka?"

Tre yelled, "Nobody, just us!"

I signaled Mula and Sweets to search the house.

"Good!" I said, dumping the other two niggas down that laid next to him.

We were in the middle of the hood. I knew somebody had to hear the shots. So, I figured we had less than five minutes before the police or anybody else showed up.

"Tre, you wanna live? You got five seconds to tell me where the money and the dope at."

He said, "Fuck you, niggaz. I ain't givin' y'all shit" He spit on my boot.

"What?" I said. "Oh, yeah?" Then I said in my normal voice, "You're a cocky nigga, huh?"

He looked up at me and his eyes lit up in recognition. I put the barrel of my gun to the back of his head and pulled the trigger. Back in Moo mode, I yelled, "Three minutes and fifteen seconds!"

***

Mula

Creeping up the stairs, my heart was beating so hard I thought it was going to come out of my chest. *Calm down, bitch. Stay focused,* I told myself. Once the gunfire ceased, it was pure silence. Wait, I think I heard something in the room to my right, fuck. I put my back to the wall, twisted the doorknob, and slowly pushed the door open. I peeked inside the room twice. The first time, I couldn't believe my eyes. I peeked again.

The small room had a table and chairs inside and nothing else I could see besides a closet. The table, however, had stacks of money on it, covering it all the way across. Fuck it! I swung in, guns up. I was startled by the sound of movement again, with both guns pointed at the closet, I paused. Then I heard a scratching sound and whimpering. I glanced around the room once more, noticing a bag of Puppy Chow and a dog bowl in the far, right corner.

I had to be sure, I cautiously opened the closet door and a grey, female pitbull puppy came running out with a muzzle on its head. Bricks were neatly stacked on the shelf above. I didn't waste another second. I took my bag and quickly filled it with money and the dope. The dog didn't growl at me or anything. It just sat there and watched me.

I heard Hood yell, "Thirty seconds! Find that shit and let's go!" Her voice made me jump a lil' bit.

I gotta get used to this manly-ass voice she using, I told myself. I zipped up the bag and threw it over my shoulder. That bitch was heavy. I looked at the dog sitting there staring at me and I said, "Tu-tu-tu—come on—we out!" She followed. I ran down the hallway and hit the stairs with her right on my heels. "I got it!" I yelled, coming down the stairs and finally reaching the landing.

Lue asked, "What the fuck is that?" She was looking down at the puppy.

"Aw, that's Scratches," I said, I had already decided on a name for her.

"Fuck that, time!" Hood clapped her hands and we got up out that bitch—leaving nothing breathing.

"P.Y.T., wait till y'all see what we got!" I told them as we pulled from the curb.

K'ajji

Chapter 42

Gina

1:35 a.m.

Tired, yawning, and shit, I turned off my siren as I pulled up on about a dozen officers. This was supposed to be my day off but, so much for that. I got the call so here I am on 32nd in Burleigh. Somebody had gotten themself killed. I got out of my car and was greeted by Sergeant Jamison.

"Cakes, sweetheart, you look terrible. Were you sleepin'?" He laughed.

"Tuh, fuck you very much. And if you really must know, yeah, my ass was sleep!" I said, sliding on my latex gloves. "Bring me up to speed. What we got? Why you tryin' to be funny?" I smiled.

"Well, you remember the scene on Locust a few weeks ago?"

"Yeah, of course, 28th."

"That's the one. Here's the thing, it looks pretty much like that one, horrific. We got four dead. The M.E.'s inside—"

"What! What that bitch doin' workin' my crime scene? You know I don't like nobody fuckin' with my shit!"

"Well, we called you twenty minutes ago. Initially, I held her off, but, she kind of insisted." He raised his arms in a gesture of defeat.

"Well, politely go yo' ass up on that porch and call her ass up outta there. Now!"

"Jeez, break my balls why don't cha. Relax, I'll take care of it, okay?" he replied as he walked off. He kept looking back, inviting a response.

"Hmph!" I just crossed my arms and looked at him.

He knew damn well me and this hoe had animosity ever since she tried to override my dialect and theory on a murder that happened two years ago. Ever since then *Miss Jenna* had been doing her investigations down at the Medical Examiner's Office where that ass belonged. Why she decided to bring her white ass to the hood today, I don't know. But she'd better get her lil' shit and get gone, or I was taking my ass back home and going to sleep!

Hell, I ain't got time for the bullshit, I'm thinking as I leaned against my car.

She came out of the house and I saw Jamison say something to her, pointing at me. She rolled her eyes and I was hoping she would say something slick. They were walking towards me.

"Uh-huh, bring yo' ass here!" The skank had the nerve to smile as I wagged my finger.

"Oh, Burke, I know you're upset but—"

"But my ass! Did you touch anything?"

"Noooo, I swear." She held up her right hand.

"Put your damn hand down. This ain't court. You need to leave. You're no longer needed here. You'll get the bodies when they get to you. Bye!" I waved her off and started walking towards my scene.

Then I heard her say, "Black women."

I turned around, walked back to her, and got right up in her face. I said, "Uh-huh, and you can kiss my black muthafuckin' ass, too, Jenna! I heard yo' punk-ass! Oh yeah, give me dis!" I snatched her flashlight out her hand and walked off.

Jenna said, "But that's—"

"Yeah, yeah bitch! I'll mail it to you when I'm done!"

She was pissed, she got into her lil' car and sped off.

I said, "Jay, canvass the area!" Bitch fuckin' with my pension.

As I walked up onto the porch, I noticed a shotgun shell to my right. The lock on the door had been blown off. The door itself was barely on its hinges.

"McCloud!" I called out to one of the white-boy rookies standing outside his patrol car, looking like he was about to shit bricks, seeing all the black folk out there.

"Yeah!"

"Look in my glove compartment, pop the trunk, and bring me my evidence case. I need bags!" I yelled.

"Gotcha! No problem, Burke!" he yelled, jumping at the opportunity to help.

"Thank you," I replied as he ran to my car.

He brought me my kit and the first thing I did was collect that spent shell, hoping for at least a half print. When I stepped into the house, there were three bodies right there in the living room in the middle of the floor. They were shot execution-style just like the victims on Locust as Jamison had said. They were all shot in the head and backs with a .45 caliber weapon. They hadn't stood a chance. This was a drug house. It had that distinctive odor, I could tell by its lack of furniture as well. It had no woman's touch whatsoever.

I checked my first victims for IDs, I found cash and more cash as expected. Jivontre Tre-Rida Jordan, Dontrell Lil' Trell Curtis, and Ryan Church Bailey all laid before me dead. There was another body lying in the doorway of one of the bedrooms. I made my way to him, I saw two wounds in his upper back and one in his lower.

Damn, it was Fly as the streets knew him. His real name was Kevin Isby and he was only seventeen. Just to be sure he was gone, I checked for a pulse and I'll be damned.

"We got a live one! I got one alive!" I yelled. "Get me an ambulance nowww!"

Then he moved, he was conscious. Fly opened his eyes and looked right at me. "Get me some fuckin' help in heereee! Baby, don't move. Hear me? Stay still." I'm thinking, *Moo-Moo and Doe I finally got y 'all ass.*

"Freddy," Fly mumbles, coughing up blood.

I told him to save his energy. "Shhhh, don't try to speak. Help is comin'." All the while I'm racking my brain. *Who the fuck is Freddy?*

K'ajji

Chapter 43

Zoo

Me and Goodie were lying in the bed, chilling, when I got a call from the lil' chic, Zanita out in the hood, telling me the police were deep down on tre-deuce. I called a few of my niggas and we headed that way. When we got there the entire block was standing outside the spot, trying to see what was going on. It looked as if they had half the precinct out here. Spotting Burke's Crown, I knew that could mean only one thing and the word, *murder* traveled fast. Nigga's entire families started pulling up, mommas, grandmamas, sisters, and aunties. Everybody had questions that none of us had sure answers to.

The only nigga I knew for sure to likely be up in there was Tre because this was his spot. His aunt and sister were out here, going through it. When the ambulance pulled up, and they rushed my nigga Fly out, I couldn't do anything but shake my head. Not another one of mine. Famo and Blue had just come home, one paralyzed and the other with one arm and one lung.

Burke came out with the stretcher, barking orders. "Seal this crime scene! I don't want nobody in there! I'm goin' with 'em. Jamison, this is Kevin Isby! Notify his family, tell 'em to meet us at Froedert! Got it?"

"I'm on it, Burke!" replied the big cracker.

Although many stayed out of concern for those they loved who were possibly in that house, there wasn't much more left for me to see. Anybody else inside had to be dead. So me, U-Tee and Proof dipped and headed for the hospital. If we were to get any answers, they would hopefully come from Fly.

***

Inside the Ambulance

"Fr-Freddy—" Fly mumbled.

"His vital signs are low!" one EMT yelled.

"We got three gunshots!" another EMT said.

"He's lost a lot of blood!" the first EMT yelled.

"Will he make it?" Gina asked.

"Chances are low," one EMT answered. "If you need to ask him anything, ask him now!"

A cold sweat had formed on his skin, his eyes fluttered, and his jaws were clenched, they were losing him. "Is that who shot chu? What's his last name?"Gina held his hand. "Damn it! Kevin! Kevin."

Th-they had on—it hurts—" Fly paused, then tried to speak again.

"Whatchu say, baby?" Gina leaned in. It was hard for her to hear because of the siren's blare.

"Fre-Freddy Krueger. They had on Freddy Krueger masks." His chest heaved.

"How many were there?"

"Five—"

"There were five?" she asked for confirmation. He shook his head, yes. "Was it the twins? Kevin was it Moo-Moo and Doe-Doe? Talk to me."

"He's spiking! Move back! Move back!" one of the EMTs pushed Gina aside.

**

Fly's sisters, Kyra and Angel, and his mother, Missy, rushed into the ER and headed straight for me.

"Zoo, where my baby? What happened?" his mother asked.

"They brought him in a few minutes ago. Somethin' happened at the spot. He was over there with Tre. That's all I know."

"Well, what they say? How is he?" Kyra tearfully asked. She was the youngest.

"I don't know. They won't give us no information bein' we ain't family," I replied.

They rushed the receptionist. However, she could only tell them that he was brought in with three gunshot wounds to his back. Burke came out minutes later and they drove down on her as well. She pulled them to the side and sat them down. She and Missy had attended high school together so they were on a first-name basis.

"Gina, how bad is it? What happened?"

"Missy-Mae, he was shot three—three times," Gina cautiously replied.

"I know, I know is he—"

"I—I—I rode with 'em Mae, Mae—Mae, don't worry. He gon' be alright." Gina's eyes said she was lying and Missy saw it.

"Gina, don't bullshit me! How bad is he?"

"It's bad, but—"

"Oh, my God!" Missy broke down crying as more of the hood poured into the emergency room entrance.

"What happened?" Missy yelled.

Gina just hugged her. Finally, the doctor came out and asked to see the family. Missy, wrapped in Gina's arms, had her back to him. Gina raised her hand and the doctor walked over to them. When Missy fell to her knees I knew my nigga didn't make it. Everybody was on some revenge shit. I felt stupid because I'd told them I made an agreement with 3C and shit was straight.

Now, I had to convince them to stay calm while we asked some questions to find out what went down. My mind went to the same shit theirs did. I'd been double-crossed. The next day I went by Missy's crib to give my condolences as well as to see if Burke had told his mom anything. She said Burke hadn't been straightforward with her at first because it was an ongoing investigation. But after a while, she gave it up to her old buddy. Burke said Fly told her five niggas wearing Freddy Krueger masks ran up in the spot.

I went straight home and called the number the twins had just given me only hours before. Doe answered the phone.

"Hello!" I yelled.

"What up, this Doe."

"What up, nigga! I thought we had a muthafuckin' deal! That lil' shit y'all got ain't nothin' compared to what y'all had comin'!"

"Who dis? Zoo, what the fuck you talkin' about, nigga?"

"I'm talkin' about y'all runnin' up in the spot last night and killin' folks 'nem, nigga! Do the Freddy masks sound familiar, huh?"

"Listen, lil' nigga! I don't know what the fuck you talkin' 'bout, or who you gotcha info from! If a muthafucka got it last night I guarantee you, it didn't come from our end! Ain't nobody from 3C have shit to do with it!"

"You tellin' me y'all ain't run in Tre-Rida spot in Freddy Krueger masks?"

"It sounds like some shit we'd do, but hell nall, nigga! Y'all got other problems y'all obviously ain't know nothin' about! What up? We stay ready, locked, and loaded! However, you wanna do this shit. You say you wanna end this shit." The phone went silent.

Zoo said, "I'll get back at you."

"Yeah, you do that!" Doe slammed the phone down.

Chapter 44

The Twins

Moo laughed as he reclined in the leather love seat, playing a video game. "Damn, niggaz get killed and niggaz automatically blame us, huh?" Doe said, "Yeah, but listen to this, Zoo say mufuckaz done ran up in Tre-Rida shit dressed like Freddy." Moo paused the game and sat up in the chair. "What? Dressed like—you thinkin' what I'm thinkin'?" "Yup, that's why I'm callin' her ass right now." Doe dialed the crib. "Hello, hey, Tip. Tash-Tasha there? She where? A'ight, I'll be through there later on. Let me call over there, real quick. I need to holla at her. Yeah, I know the number. Love you, too. Bye." "What she say?" Moo asked, watching Doe hang up and dial another number. "She over by Brianna's. Hello, Bri, this Doe. Where my sistah at? Put her on the phone. Hello, Hood, y'all get y'all asses over here, right now! I'm hollerin' at yo' muthafuckin' ass! Mill Road! Yeah, and make sure don't nobody follow y'all dumb ass! Be here within the next fifteen minutes! Yeah, a'ight!" Doe hung up.

***

P.Y.T.

Hood

I hung the phone back on the kitchen wall and walked back into the living room where everybody was watchin' *Good Times*. "Oooh, y'all, somehow I think they know." I flopped down onto the couch. "Know what?" Sweets asked, acting dumb, barely looking up from the T.V.

"Know we hit the lick. Whatchu think?" I replied dryly.

"Why you say that?" Lue asked, smiling.

"Cause Doe pissed! He wants us to come see them, right now."

"But how would they know?" Bri asked. "Ain't none of us told nobody—"

Mula said, "We ain't been nowhere. Ain't no way."

"Well, I guess we'll see when we get there. I mean, it gotta be somethin'. They want me to take y'all to one of their spots I didn't even know about until a few weeks ago. That's not like them."

Mula said, "Well, bitch, let's go see what they want. What can they do?"

"A'ight Mu, all I gotta say is you don't know my brothers like I do. I done took plenty of ass whippings." Everybody got up.

"Well, I ain't takin' none," Mula said pulling out her keys. We left, and as we jumped into the van she said, "They would have found out anyways. You and Sweets need new burners. You know they would've asked what happened to the ones they just gave y'all.

"Damn, you right," I told her as she looked at me through the rearview mirror.

Once we were in traffic, I fiddled with my thumbs, nervous the entire way there. I thought we'd covered all our tracks. Our first mission and we'd been figured out. I couldn't believe this shit, but, it is what it is. Only a few minutes had passed, and we were pulling up in the driveway. We got out of the van, walked to the door, and rang the doorbell.

Moo answered. "Get y'all asses in here!" he yelled, standing aside, letting us in. He mugged each and every one of us as we walked past him.

Leave it to Lue's lil' ass to say something slick, "Boy, stop playin'! You ain't nobody daddy. Sheewd!"

Doe was sitting in the living room. He got up and told us to have a seat on the couch. Moo took a seat across from us as Doe paced the floor in front of us with his hands behind his back.

He said, "Before y'all lil' asses get to lyin'. We know y'all ran up in Tre-Rida shit on 32nd. What the fuck was y'all thinkin?"

"We—we ain't—" I fixed my mouth to lie but Mula cut me short.

"Hood, don't I got this," she said. "Yeah, we did it—and so what! We got more doin' it ourselves than that petty-ass ten grand y'all gave us outta a quarter mil plus!" She rolled her eyes.

My eyes got big and my mouth dropped! Doe drew back to slap the shit out of her, but Moo stopped him. Mula jumped up in fight mode.

"Nigga, I wish you would hit me! How you gon' get mad anywayz? Y'all started this shit!"

Doe pushed Moo up off him. I grabbed Mula and pulled her back down on the couch. She was fuming and so was Doe.

Moo said, "Calm down, dog! She right. Chill!"

Doe said, "I'm good—"

Moo went right in. "How much y'all get?" he asked, smiling like a proud father.

I said, "eighty gees and four bricks."

Doe asked, "How many y'all kill at the scene?"

I said, "Four."

He said, "Wrong, y'all killed three! That's the shit I'm talkin' about! I made some calls! Apparently, one of the niggaz y'all shot lived and made it to the hospital. He was shot three times. A nigga they called Fly, he's dead now though." He mugged me.

Moo said, "Now, how y'all allowed him to make it that far is beyond me. You tryin' to kill somethin', you make sure it's dead. I taught y'all that before we went in on Locust."

"What y'all do with the gunz?" Doe asked. He was pacing back and forth again.

"We dumped 'em in acid," I said proudly, looking at Moo.

"What about the Freddy masks?" Moo questioned.

"We burnt—wait—how y'all know what—"

"That's what happens when you let niggaz live to tell the story. All of Burleigh and ain't no telling who else, knows. Y'all better hope everything's good. Let me guess, y'all was in that same van that y'all in, right now? What if somebody got the plates?" Doe pointed out.

"We took 'em off," Mula said, rolling her eyes.

Bri's careless, reckless-ass mouth gon' say, "Anywayz, y'all wanna buy them bricks cause we don't need 'em."

The twins laughed but she was serious as a heart attack.

Doe said, "Daaamnn, Moo, you hearin' this shit? These lil' mufuckaz tryin' to sell us some bricks!"

The day turned into nightfall as they went on and on asking questions, *Who drove? Where we parked? How we got in? Did we split up? Who blasted what niggaz?* Moo realized right away—though it took Doe a lil' longer to grasp the fact—-we were growing up, and, that they'd created the tenacious, murderous bitches we'd become. They couldn't do shit but deal with it.

Chapter 45

Teague

One Week Later

After years of torment, agony, and pain from hearing he'd never be free again, it was a day he'd long-awaited. Teague sat quietly next to his lawyer as he performed in the courtroom. They'd been at it for over two hours and the United States District Attorney, Mario Contreras, tried his best to assure Teague would never see the streets again.

"Your Honor, at one time this man was the most notorious drug lord Milwaukee County had ever seen!"

"You have no actual proof that my client has ever sold a crumb!" Henak clapped back.

"Excuse me, your client was indicted and prosecuted! Many witnesses—"

"Witnesses that would say anything to lighten the sentences for themselves! See, Mesarosh versus The United States! It now holds that the government will not permit the conviction of any person on tainted testimony! Judge, some of these witnesses have admitted, during and after Mr. Phillups' conviction, to perjuring themselves! Your Honor, these witnesses are the worst of the worst! It's clearly established law! The Supreme Court has warned against the unholy alliances between con artist convicts who want "out" of their own cases and, law enforcement who are running the training grounds for snitches on the streets and over at the county jails! Prosecutors are simply taking what appears to be the easy route rather than putting together a case with solid evidence! It is clearly established in Crawford that snitch testimony ought not be passed upon under the same rules governing as an apparent credible witness! These sorts of witnesses are all the State has!"

"No need to get overzealous, Mr. Henak," the Judge said. "I hear you loud and clear. What does the State have to say to these accusations? Are they true? Were all the witnesses brought against this man indicted themselves and given leniency?"

"Yes!" Henak answered for him.

"Yo—Your Honor—the defense is implying that Mr. Phillups was not a drug dealer, that the witnesses against him were all liars!"

"Yes, I heard him." The judge sat back in his chair.

"All the currency confiscated by agents tested positive for narcotics!"

The judge said, "So does ninety-seven percent of the currency around this country! Jones v. DEA, eight-nineteen Federal Supplement six-ninety-eight! Did they find any drugs? You got video, audio, anything?"

"No, Your Honor," Henak interrupted. The State was spent.

The D.A. said, "Okay, enough about the indictment. The defendant shot and killed Mr. Tony Harden in cold blood!" He was on that U.S.D.A. shit, trying to gain ground.

"Ahem, excuse me." Henak took a sip of his water. He said, "Yes, I'm glad you brought it to the court's attention. Yes, my client was apprehended after shooting Mr. Harden in front of his home. And he had every right to do so. Mr. Harden raped his wife."

"Your Honor, that wasn't his wife—" Henak rummaged through his file. He'd found exactly what he was looking for.

The judge said, "I'm more interested in the charge of rape, Counselor. Whether she was his wife or not is irrelevant!"

Henak held up a piece of paper. The bailiff came and got it and handed it to the judge.

Henak said, "Common Law. They were together for more than nine years!"

"What is that?" the D.A. demanded to know.

Henak said, "Witnesses have come forward that saw my client drag Mr. Harden out of his home in the nude. There was a big struggle for the weapon then Mr. Phillups shot the victim. There is also a sworn statement provided to the court as well as the district attorney's office from Ms. Fields concerning this matter. In this statement, she's adamant that Mr. Harden raped her! Her statement never changed from day one! However, she's now deceased. The lower courts, the police department, as well as the D.A.'s office, failed to acknowledge this claim or take any actions to vindicate my client of these first-degree murder charges!"

"Is this true, Mr. Contreras? I mean, I'm looking at the statements from Ms. Niecy Fields here." The judge looked down at him over his reading glasses which sat on the tip of his nose.

"Well, yes, but—but—"

"I believe I've heard enough! Court is adjourned, I'll summon you all when I've made my decision." The judge stood up and gathered up all the evidence before him.

"But Your Honor!" Contreras pleaded.

The judge slammed his gavel down and walked into his chambers. in his holding cell, all Teague could do was wait.

***

Three Weeks Later

No call, but also no drama from Zoo and those Burleigh niggas. So, back in the hood, the twins were masked and gloved up, packaging the diesel in aluminum foil and the 'caine in Royal Seals. They were getting shit ready for their dope houses as well as the bricks for the heavy hitters. Knowing the fiends came in packs during the early morning hours, they were behind schedule. It was 12:30 in the afternoon. They heard a knock on the basement door. Bella, Telesis and Honesty were screaming their names. Moo and Doe grabbed their guns and headed upstairs to see exactly what was going on.

When they got up there, they couldn't believe who was sitting right there in their living room. It was Teague, sitting there, in a white tailored tux. They tucked their weapons.

He smiled and said, "What y'all lil' niggaz gon' do? Shoot me? Come on over here and give it up." He stood to greet his boys.

"What the fuck!" Doe smiled, taking off his mask and gloves, rushing in for the hug. "When you get out?" They embraced.

191

"Yeah!" Moo countered. "And why you ain't tell nobody?" Moo hugged him as well.

"I got out a few hours ago. Tip and Fry knew, so did these fine young ladies right here y'all introduced me to over the years. I'd asked 'em all along to keep it a secret. I didn't tell y'all about the hearing just in case it didn't go my way. I didn't want y'all to feel that disappointment. Then again, I ain't want y'all sister in there hearin' that shit about her father as the State tried to portray me as some sort of monster. I already know she feels some kind of way."

"Don't even worry about it," Moo said. "She'll be a'ight, and I bet she'll be happy to see you."

"Yeah, but let's get you outta here," Doe said. "You just comin' home. This the last place you wanna be."

Teague said, "Nall, actually, this is exactly where I need to be. What up with these niggaz?"

Moo said, "We got a plan, but first, I think we should have a sit-down. There's a lot that you need to know."

***

Doe

We drove pops out to the crib we rarely used out on 95th in Fondulac. It was already laced so we knew he'd feel more comfortable out there. He'd been gone all of sixteen years, so much had changed.

"What up? You hungry?" I asked him, taking off my jacket and hanging it up. He was looking around, sizing the place up.

"Nah, Tip already fed me." He picked up a photo off the mantelpiece. It was an old picture of him and moms in Italy, taken a long time ago. He smiled. "I see y'all been doin' good for y'all selves."

"Yeah, we do that," Moo said, flopping down on the leather sofa.

Teague said, "So, tell me everything I need to know. Operations, war, family. What up?" He put the picture back in its place, unbuttoned his blazer, and took a seat on the love seat.

I said, "Operations are up and runnin' again. As far as war—"

Moo interjected, "We got a pawn over in J.L.'s camp that's tryin' to become king." He pulled out a toothpick and stuck it in his mouth. "But the main thing we need to talk about is Hood."

I said, "She wild, pops. And it's all our fault. Yours included—"

He said, "Whatchu mean, wild? I know she got a mouth on her. But—"

"Nall, she wild as in bodyin' shit wild." I smiled.

Teague said, "What! What the hell y'all done did to my girl! Awwww shit! Don't tell me." He put his head in his hands then looked back up at us.

Moo said, "Yeah, the heat was on. I had to teach her the M-Game. Doe got hit, I needed somebody I could trust."

"I understand, but is she—she handlin' herself?" Teague asked in disbelief.

"No hesitation," Moo replied. "Number one rule, she's seasoned."

Teague said, "Well, y'all go get her. I need to holla at her anyway. I'ma stay right here. If the nigga J.L. finds out I'm out, that bitch gon' take flight, no question."

"A'ight, make yourself at home." I stood up. "There's movies, music, food—"

Moo said, "Damn, you want us to bring you back anything else while we're out? Cause we can—"

"Like what?" Teague asked in confusion.

"*Like what?* Like some pussy! You do remember what that is, don't you?" We all burst out laughing.

He waved us off. "I'll get to that soon enough. This here is more important. Besides, the next woman I lay down with gon' be special. I don't want just anything no more. Hear me?"

Moo said, "A'ight, but if you change your mind, the offer still stands."

"Appreciated. Now, gon' getcha sister."

We were on our way out the door when the phone rang, turning us around. Moo said, "It's most likely Jahnahdah. How the hell that girl always managin' to find us?" He flopped back down on the couch.

"Shut up, nigga. Don't be talkin' like my baby a stalker or some shit. I had all the calls forwarded. Hello, what up? This Doe." I covered the phone and said to Moo, "You just mad ain't nobody callin' yo' ass. Hello, my bad." I tapped Moo so he could read my lips, *"This Zoo."* I pointed at the phone. "Yeah—when, tonight? Aw, okay. Hell yeah. You know where the old mill at? Ex—exactly, that's three days. We want him there by a quarter to twelve. Yeah, shit we was startin' to think you was on bullshit. We hadn't heard from you in a while. But check this out, if anything looks outta place. A'ight now, I hear you. So, whatchu got planned on your end of this soldier?"

I listened to what Zoo had to say with an open mind. It sounded solid. He said the only thing which was stalling his plan was that J.L.'s shipment hadn't landed. It should be there within two days. We were to be ready to go in three. I told Moo and pops what was said and we left to go grab Hood. Things didn't go so well with her and Teague. Despite his efforts to make amends, she wasn't trying to hear it. She ran up out of the crib and before we could catch up with her, she'd disappeared into the night.

Teague said, "Just give it some time. She's got the right to feel the way she feels. She loves me, she just don't know how to admit it. Hell. I'm the only thing she's ever known as far as a father figure. She don't understand my pain. I loved that nigga! She ain't never known that man!" He shook his head. "That muthafucka!" he said, thinking of years past. He was still pissed at his dead homie.

Chapter 46

Zoo

It was time to put the plan into motion. Me and U-Tee pulled into the long driveway that led to Unk's and Cuppy's mansion down on Lake Drive. She was still out in Jamaica, so I knew he was home alone. Absolutely nobody was to be brought out here to the main pad. He'd told me not to come here, but fuck 'em. I dipped right up to the front door, got out, and rang the doorbell. If he didn't know I was out here by his pit bulls barking and acting a damn fool, he knew now.

I rang the shit outta that bell until he came to the door in his pajamas.

"Zoo, what the fuck you doin' here?" he asked as I barged past him. He looked out the door. "Who—who that in the—"

"That's Tee, I know you told me to never come down here, but I got so excited all that shit went out the window. I told you we was gon' handle them niggaz!"

"Whatchu talkin' 'bout?"

"Come on, get dressed. You need to come with us. We got them niggaz, Unk!"

"Who? The twins, y'all got the twins?"

"Yeah, throw somethin' on real quick! Here." I handed him the .9mm off my waist.

He cocked it. "Shit, I can go like this. Let me grab my coat real quick." He walked to a closet and grabbed a black trench coat.

"Where y'all got 'em at?"

"We got 'em wrapped up off Capitol."

"They dead?" he asked, sliding his arms into the sleeves of the trench.

"Nall, we took 'em alive." We walked outside and jumped in the four-door, big-body 'Lac.

J.L. said, "With the shit we just got last night, once we kill these niggaz, everything should be back on track." He was still thinking about nothing but his money.

***

Hood

The courts tried to sweep the shit under the rug. Nobody but 3C and immediate family knew Teague was out. Shit, I didn't even know until they tried to surprise me. Now here we go again. They came and got me, talking about another duck-off. They were acting all strange and jittery and shit. They kept checking behind us and acting real secretive, had my ass feeling like I was being kidnapped.

"Where the hell y'all taking me?" I yelled in frustration. It was damn near midnight and I was tired. But here I am, in all black, with my two old ladies.

Doe replied, "Just shut up and ride!"

Moo drove in silence, I didn't feel like arguing so, I just kicked back and listened to the music.

"Don 't push me cause I'm close to the eeedge/
I'm tryin' not to lose my head/ Hu-hu-hu-hu-hu!
It's like a jungle sometimes it makes me wonder/
How I keep from goin' under—" Grand Master Flash was spittin' that fire through the speakers.

I couldn't help but sing along. Soon we were pulling up to A.O. Smith, the old steel mill off 32nd in Capitol. I couldn't also help but wonder, what the fuck we were doing here? Doe opened a black duffel bag.

He turned to me in the back seat and said, "Here, put this on." He handed me a black ski mask.

I put it on. We got out and walked inside. It was kind of spooky in there and all dark. Wasn't shit in there but a whole bunch of spider webs and old machinery. As we walked through the mill we turned a corner and saw more masked men in all black, standing around these two chairs which sat under this lone light fixture. I was a little taken aback so I grabbed Moo's hoodie.

He said, "It's a'ight, just come on."

The dudes standing around in all black had what I always refer to as *them army guns*. Moo and Doe sat down in the chairs and two dudes started tying their hands behind their backs.

"Wait a minute! What the fuck goin' on here?" I asked, clutching that iron, ready to dump if needed. I was confused.

Moo said, "Stay calm. We supposed to look like we've been taken captive."

"But as you can see, everybody here is with us," Doe finished his sentence.

"This me girl." Telesis lifted her mask so I could see her face.

She was one of the people tying them up. Wintress, Yetta, Honesty, Jilla, and Tank all sounded off, letting me know they were there. That gave me comfort.

Doe said, "Hood, soon three dudes gon' come through them doors. No need to worry. Two of 'em with us. The third will be the target."

Moo said, "Just follow our lead and stand there with yo' gunz pointed at us, a'ight?"

"Here they come, they just pulled up!" I heard a loud voice yell from above, causing me to look up.

***

J. L. unsuspectingly got out the car and walked into the factory, paying little attention to the nigga standing outside the mill's doors holding an AK, thinking he was amongst his own. He marched in like he was king, unbeknownst to what awaited him. Zoo and U-Tee fell in by his sides.

He said, "Where they bitch-ass at?" As he looked around the abandoned building.

As planned, Zoo said, "Proof, lead the way."

Posing as Zoo's ally, Six didn't say a word. He just nodded and led them through the darkened maze. J.L. pulled the .9mm Zoo had given him as he rounded the corner. He could see the twins in the distance, alive and bound, just as Zoo had promised.

"I wanna kill these lil' muthafuckaz myself!" he yelled, walking in their direction.

Standing directly in front of them, he said, "Yeeahhh, what up! Long time no see, and we finally meet again. Tell me, how do it feel knowin' you 'bout to die?"

Moo smiled and said, "I don't know. How you feelin' right now, nigga?" He chuckled. "You can't feel it?"

J.L. said, "Whatchu say young dog! Y'all in a pretty fucked up position here! And you still talkin' shit, huh? Which one is you anywayz? I can't tell y'all lil' black asses apart, never could." He leaned in.

Moo spit his toothpick in his face. "Moo, nigga!"

"Aw, okay." He wiped his face. "Moo-Moo wanna be the first to die then!" J.L. attempted to raise his gun but felt the barrel of Zoo's .44 pressed against his ear. Zoo cocked the hammer back.

"Zoo, what the fuck you doin?" he asked, holding the .9mm.

"Ain't no firin' pin in it, Unk! You might as well drop that shit you stupid, greedy mufucka! All you had to do was pay these niggaz! I should blow yo' mufuckin' brains out!"

J.L. swung his gun around, pulling the trigger, trying to kill Zoo. *Click! Click! Click! Click!* "Neph—I—I—" He dropped the gun and raised his hands.

"Shut the fuck up! I ain't gon' kill yo' ass. It's a few niggaz here that's gon' do that for me."

That's when Teague walked up, holding an AR-15. He peeled off his mask, breathing heavily, trying to contain his anger. Even Lil' Zoo was surprised to see him in the flesh. J.L.'s bitch-ass nutted up.

"Tea—Te—Teague—look, man! I was gone—"

"Shhhhhh!" Teague hushed him, staring him in his eyes as he slowly untied the twins. Teague said, "Hood, come over here!" She walked over to them, a .45 in each hand. Teague gently pulled off her mask. He wanted to see her eyes.

"I took somethin' from you that can never be replaced," Teague told her. "Love is powerful, it causes many things. I know you said

198

you don't fuck with me, and I won't force you to do so. I understand. You still bitter about what I did. But, like I told you a few days ago, I'm here and I'll be your father if you allow me to. Grip was a friend of mine that betrayed my trust. He touched someone that was truly sacred to me. He ain't comin' back, but here I am.

"I love you because you're a part of your mother. You're also a part of him that has never wronged me. Now, before you left, I promised to always be here for you. You know me. You've known me! You know the real me when they'd taken everything from me and all I had was my word. My word is bond. In this life, be careful with whom you share your love with.

"Because love can cause you to be selfish as I once was. It ain't all about me. I ask that you forgive me and accept this gift as one of many to come." He looked at J. L. "This the nigga right here that killed y'all, momma. I wanted 'em for myself. But y'all have y'all way with 'em."

Zoo said, "Make sure it's messy like we agreed. That's my cue. We out, I'll call y'all in the mornin' with that location to come get y'all bricks. The money is in the car. Have y'all niggaz pull it in and strip it."

J.L. began to plead for his life as Zoo and U-Tee were escorted out the building. "Teague, please, I'm a multimillionaire! I got houses, mansions all over the world! A villa in Jamaica! Yachts and cars, I—I—you can have it all, baby! Nephew, Zoo, Don't leave meee!" he cried.

Teague said, "Somebody please kill this bitch!" He walked towards the exit J.L. fell to his knees.

Doe said, "A'ight, everybody out! We got it from here!"

Hood said, "Teague!" He stopped and turned around in the midst of the 3C soldiers exiting the building. She said, "Thank you! I love you, too! And—I forgive you!"

He smiled but kept it moving. "I'll be outside, baby girl!" he yelled. "Take y'all time!"

"Nooo, wait!" She ran to him and hugged him .45s in hand. Breaking their embrace, she tucked one of her guns.

She took him by the hand and began walking him back. "You promised to always be here for me, right? Well, we gon' do this here together, daddy." She smiled.

Moo rolled out a table and Doe opened the duffel bags. "Unk, guess what?" Doe said, looking at J.L. on his knees praying. "Your other nephew wants you found, piece-by-piece, throughout Burleigh. Ain't that a bitch? Gotta grant his wishes."

Moo said, "Show 'em what we workin' with."

"Why certainly," Doe said with a smile.

First, he pulled out a hacksaw and two butcher knives. Then he pulled out a buzz saw and two scalpels. Saving the best for last, he pulled out the chainsaw. It was the very same make and model J.L. had his folks use on Too Deep, Lil' Joshie, and countless others. He'd bought dozens of them. They dragged him to his feet and tied him to one of the chairs. Showing no mercy, they went to work on him. His whimpers as he was tied up soon became screams. They made sure he'd die a slow and painful death—all in the name of Intimate.

Chapter 47

The Present

So, Ms. Tasha *2 Hood* Phillups, how do you feel about your story?"
Bri asked, faking as if she was giving Hood an exclusive interview,
holding her empty flute like a mic.

"What up, this ya girl, Hood and I give you damn near my
whole life story just in case you got questions on why I am how I
am. Why a bitch do what she do? This that P.Y.T. shit and as you
can see—nah, I wasn't turned out. A bitch was raised this way. Love
me or hate me. The crazy thing about it is we ain't done yet!"

"Let's get this muthafuckin' money!"

"Damn bitch! Pass the damn weed. You can't say you ain't hoggin'."

"Here Mula! You trippin'. I was jus—"

"Just smokin' all the damn weed up." Bri rolled her eyes.

Lue said, "She hit that shit about ten times."

"Yo' lil' ass countin' my puffs?"

"Nah, but still—" Lue smiled.

"You, hoes is turnin' into some straight-up weed heads,"
Sweets said, rolling up another one.

Bri said, "Shit, look who's talkin'."

Sweets said, "What—" Firin' up the next one.

"Wait a minute. Shhhh, y'all hear that—" I paused.

"Hood, now you trippin'." Mula took a toke of the weed.

"Nah, bitch, for real." I jumped up and peeked out the window.
"It's the pol—"

Booom! They burst in deep! *SWAT!* Everything seemed to be
moving in slow motion.

"M.P.D.! Everybody dowwwn!"

"Police!"

"Hands! Hands! Let me see your fuckin' hands! She got a gun!
Gun! Gun! Gun! Gun!"

I tried to stop her. I yelled, "Sweets, noooo! Don't—"

Boom! Boom! Boom! Boom! It was too late, they shot her up.

Lue screamed, fucking me up even more. "Nooo! Y'all killed her! Y'all bitches killed heeer! Noooo! Sweeets! Sweets, get up! Get uuup!"

Sweets' eyes were wide open, and her body was lifeless. Those hoes still slapped cuffs on her. My entire body quaked. They had all of us stretched out on my living room floor, crying. That's when the bitch that vowed to get us walked in.

"She dead?" she asked one of the other officers. He nodded, confirming that my bitch was gone. "Good." She took off her shades. "Now, which one of you lil' bitches killed my daughter!"

Mula spoke, "Fuck yo' daughter bitch! I don't—"

I cut her off. "Mula, don't say nothin'! Don't nobody say nothin'!" I yelled.

This police hoe was bent on revenge. She wouldn't get us like that, not that easy. She said, "That's right! Y'all got the right to remain silent! Anything y'all say can, and will be used against you in a court of law! You have a right to an attorney when being questioned!"

I personally wasn't trying to hear shit! All I could think about was killing this bitch! Call it evil or whatever, it's just the way I felt. They had touched one of mine. Blame my heart. Don't blame my mind.

To Be Continued...
The Streets Will Never Close 2
Coming Soon!

Glossary

A
Ain't — not or no
A'iight — all right
Aye — the letter "A"
B
Bae — your significant other
Betcha - bet you
Bird — kilo of cocaine
Bodyin'- killing a person or people
Bogish — bogus, fake, out of line
Bones — herringbone necklace
Brah, Bruh, Bro' — brother
Burner — a gun
Buss ~ to bust; to shoot or make a move; take action
Butter- Fine
C
Cannon — a gun
Chop shit — to talk, kick it
Chu ~ you
Cold ~ fine, beautiful, to like something: song, woman, car, etc.
Copping — buying
Crib — house, apartment
Cuff — to conceal
Cuz — cousin
D
Da — the
Dat — that
Dayum ~ damn
Dem ~ them
Demos-product
Dip-off — to leave
Dis — this; to criticize or insult

Dog — a person; male figure

Dope — excellent, outstanding; narcotic

Drive, Drove-down » to approach

Dump — to shoot

E

Erry — every

Errybody ~ everybody

F

Fa show W for sure

Flashing — blasting

Flexing — showing out

Finna — about to

Fitty — fifty

Flicks — pictures; movies

Fly ~ beautiful, pretty

Fo'em — for them or him

Foe-five - .45 caliber

Foe-foe - .44 caliber

Fie — something is "fire" good; you like it (also Fya)

G

"G" — a gangster

Geez — thousands

Geh- give

Good-good — good weed or sex

Gotchu — got you

Grind — to hustle

Grits — grams of a controlled substance

H

Holla — to talk to, to yell

Homi — short for homicide

Hongry — hungry

Horn — telephone

Horse — heroin

Hubbaz ~ big rocks of cocaine (made famous by

U.G.K.)
Hype — a drug addict
I
I'ont –I don't
Iron — a gun
J
Jackin' e Slick talk; to talk shit
J ump-Out-Boyz - a police task force assigned
specifically to hunt men of color in urban
communities
L
Look-a-Whoin' - being nosey
Lac ~ Cadillac
M
Mash — drive; to speed
Merch — short for merchandise
M-Game — murder game; how to kill
Mo' — more
Muggin' — to look at another with hate or anger
Murda — murder
N
Nah — no
Nall — no
N aw - no
'Nem — them
Nigga — men of color: Never Ignorant, Getting Goals
Accomplished (made famous by 2Pac
Shakur)
Nina — .9mn1 caliber weapon
Nuggets — gold nugget rings
O
Old-Head — older peer, old man
On "S" — to be on security
Outta - out of

P
Paper — money
Pop — soda; to shoot
R
Reppin' — representing
S
Scratches — money
Screw-face — looking angry
Shorty — a young child; a beautiful woman
Sistah — sister
Stab-out — to drive away with haste
Strap- A gun
Stroll - to walk
Sum-ta-ya — something to you
Sweet — soft
Swerve — a drug addict; a customer
Sweat A to harass
T
Ta — to
Taiight - tonight, with a mouthful
Thangz — guns
Thump, Thumper - a gun or guns
Tip — house or apartment
Tool - a gun
Trap — an old vehicle not in the best condition
True-dat — that's true
U
Unit - a gun
W
Whatchu - what you
Whip — a nice car
Wit - with
Wanna, Wonna — want to
Y

Y'all — you all
Yo' — your
Young-Dog — young man

Submission Guideline

Submit the first three chapters of your completed manuscript to ldpsubmissions@gmail.com, subject line: Your book's title. The manuscript must be in a .doc file and sent as an attachment. Document should be in Times New Roman, double spaced and in size 12 font. Also, provide your synopsis and full contact information. If sending multiple submissions, they must each be in a separate email.

Have a story but no way to send it electronically? You can still submit to LDP/Ca$h Presents. Send in the first three chapters, written or typed, of your completed manuscript to:

LDP: Submissions Dept
Po Box 944
Stockbridge, Ga 30281

DO NOT send original manuscript. Must be a duplicate.

Provide your synopsis and a cover letter containing your full contact information.

Thanks for considering LDP and Ca$h Presents.

The Streets Will Never Close

BOW DOWN TO MY GANGSTA

By **Ca$h**

TORN BETWEEN TWO

By **Coffee**

THE STREETS STAINED MY SOUL **II**

By **Marcellus Allen**

BLOOD OF A BOSS **VI**

SHADOWS OF THE GAME II

By **Askari**

LOYAL TO THE GAME **IV**

By **T.J. & Jelissa**

A DOPEBOY'S PRAYER **II**

By **Eddie "Wolf" Lee**

IF LOVING YOU IS WRONG... **III**

By **Jelissa**

TRUE SAVAGE **VII**

MIDNIGHT CARTEL III

DOPE BOY MAGIC IV

CITY OF KINGZ II

By **Chris Green**

BLAST FOR ME **III**

A SAVAGE DOPEBOY III

CUTTHROAT MAFIA III

By **Ghost**

A HUSTLER'S DECEIT III

KILL ZONE **II**

BAE BELONGS TO ME III

A DOPE BOY'S QUEEN III

K'ajji

By **Aryanna**
COKE KINGS V
KING OF THE TRAP II
By **T.J. Edwards**
GORILLAZ IN THE BAY V
De'Kari
THE STREETS ARE CALLING II
Duquie Wilson
KINGPIN KILLAZ IV
STREET KINGS III
PAID IN BLOOD III
CARTEL KILLAZ IV
DOPE GODS III
Hood Rich
SINS OF A HUSTLA II
ASAD
KINGZ OF THE GAME V
Playa Ray
SLAUGHTER GANG IV
RUTHLESS HEART IV
By **Willie Slaughter**
THE HEART OF A SAVAGE III
By **Jibril Williams**
FUK SHYT II
By **Blakk Diamond**
THE REALEST KILLAZ III
By **Tranay Adams**
TRAP GOD III
By **Troublesome**
YAYO IV

The Streets Will Never Close

A SHOOTER'S AMBITION III

By S. Allen

GHOST MOB

Stilloan Robinson

KINGPIN DREAMS III

By Paper Boi Rari

CREAM

By Yolanda Moore

SON OF A DOPE FIEND III

By Renta

FOREVER GANGSTA II

GLOCKS ON SATIN SHEETS III

By Adrian Dulan

LOYALTY AIN'T PROMISED II

By Keith Williams

THE PRICE YOU PAY FOR LOVE II

By Destiny Skai

CONFESSIONS OF A GANGSTA II

By Nicholas Lock

I'M NOTHING WITHOUT HIS LOVE II

By Monet Dragun

LIFE OF A SAVAGE IV

A GANGSTA'S QUR'AN II

MURDA SEASON II

GANGLAND CARTEL II

By **Romell Tukes**

QUIET MONEY III

THUG LIFE II

By **Trai'Quan**

THE STREETS MADE ME III

K'ajji

By **Larry D. Wright**
THE ULTIMATE SACRIFICE VI
IF YOU CROSS ME ONCE II
ANGEL III
By **Anthony Fields**
THE LIFE OF A HOOD STAR
By **Ca$h & Rashia Wilson**
FRIEND OR FOE II
By **Mimi**
SAVAGE STORMS II
By **Meesha**
BLOOD ON THE MONEY II
By **J-Blunt**
THE STREETS WILL NEVER CLOSE II
By **K'ajji**

Available Now

RESTRAINING ORDER **I & II**
By **CA$H & Coffee**
LOVE KNOWS NO BOUNDARIES **I II & III**
By **Coffee**
RAISED AS A GOON I, II, III & IV
BRED BY THE SLUMS I, II, III
BLAST FOR ME I & II
ROTTEN TO THE CORE I II III

A BRONX TALE I, II, III

DUFFEL BAG CARTEL I II III IV

HEARTLESS GOON I II III IV

A SAVAGE DOPEBOY I II

HEARTLESS GOON I II III

DRUG LORDS I II III

CUTTHROAT MAFIA I II

By **Ghost**

LAY IT DOWN **I & II**

LAST OF A DYING BREED

BLOOD STAINS OF A SHOTTA I & II III

By **Jamaica**

LOYAL TO THE GAME I II III

LIFE OF SIN I, II III

By **TJ & Jelissa**

BLOODY COMMAS I & II

SKI MASK CARTEL I II & III

KING OF NEW YORK I II,III IV V

RISE TO POWER I II III

COKE KINGS I II III IV

BORN HEARTLESS I II III IV

KING OF THE TRAP

By **T.J. Edwards**

IF LOVING HIM IS WRONG…I & II

LOVE ME EVEN WHEN IT HURTS I II III

By **Jelissa**

WHEN THE STREETS CLAP BACK I & II III

THE HEART OF A SAVAGE I II

By **Jibril Williams**

A DISTINGUISHED THUG STOLE MY HEART I II & III

K'ajji

LOVE SHOULDN'T HURT I II III IV
RENEGADE BOYS I II III IV
PAID IN KARMA I II III
SAVAGE STORMS
By **Meesha**
A GANGSTER'S CODE I &, II III
A GANGSTER'S SYN I II III
THE SAVAGE LIFE I II III
CHAINED TO THE STREETS I II III
BLOOD ON THE MONEY
By J-Blunt
PUSH IT TO THE LIMIT
By **Bre' Hayes**
BLOOD OF A BOSS **I, II, III, IV, V**
SHADOWS OF THE GAME
By **Askari**
THE STREETS BLEED MURDER **I, II & III**
THE HEART OF A GANGSTA I II& III
By **Jerry Jackson**
CUM FOR ME I II III IV V
An **LDP Erotica Collaboration**
BRIDE OF A HUSTLA **I II & II**
THE FETTI GIRLS **I, II& III**
CORRUPTED BY A GANGSTA I, II III, IV
BLINDED BY HIS LOVE
THE PRICE YOU PAY FOR LOVE
DOPE GIRL MAGIC I II III
By **Destiny Skai**
WHEN A GOOD GIRL GOES BAD
By **Adrienne**

The Streets Will Never Close

THE COST OF LOYALTY I II III
By Kweli
A GANGSTER'S REVENGE **I II III & IV**
THE BOSS MAN'S DAUGHTERS I II III IV V
A SAVAGE LOVE **I & II**
BAE BELONGS TO ME I II
A HUSTLER'S DECEIT I, II, III
WHAT BAD BITCHES DO I, II, III
SOUL OF A MONSTER I II III
KILL ZONE
A DOPE BOY'S QUEEN I II
By **Aryanna**
A KINGPIN'S AMBITON
A KINGPIN'S AMBITION **II**
I MURDER FOR THE DOUGH
By **Ambitious**
TRUE SAVAGE I II III IV V VI
DOPE BOY MAGIC I, II, III
MIDNIGHT CARTEL I II
CITY OF KINGZ
By **Chris Green**
A DOPEBOY'S PRAYER
By **Eddie "Wolf" Lee**
THE KING CARTEL **I, II & III**
By **Frank Gresham**
THESE NIGGAS AIN'T LOYAL **I, II & III**
By **Nikki Tee**
GANGSTA SHYT **I II &III**
By **CATO**
THE ULTIMATE BETRAYAL

By **Phoenix**

BOSS'N UP **I , II & III**

By **Royal Nicole**

I LOVE YOU TO DEATH

By Destiny J

I RIDE FOR MY HITTA

I STILL RIDE FOR MY HITTA

By **Misty Holt**

LOVE & CHASIN' PAPER

By **Qay Crockett**

TO DIE IN VAIN

SINS OF A HUSTLA

By **ASAD**

BROOKLYN HUSTLAZ

By **Boogsy Morina**

BROOKLYN ON LOCK I & II

By **Sonovia**

GANGSTA CITY

By **Teddy Duke**

A DRUG KING AND HIS DIAMOND I & II III

A DOPEMAN'S RICHES

HER MAN, MINE'S TOO I, II

CASH MONEY HO'S

By Nicole Goosby

TRAPHOUSE KING **I II & III**

KINGPIN KILLAZ I II III

STREET KINGS I II

PAID IN BLOOD **I II**

CARTEL KILLAZ I II III

DOPE GODS I II

The Streets Will Never Close

By **Hood Rich**
LIPSTICK KILLAH **I, II, III**
CRIME OF PASSION I II & III
FRIEND OR FOE
By **Mimi**
STEADY MOBBN' **I, II, III**
THE STREETS STAINED MY SOUL
By **Marcellus Allen**
WHO SHOT YA **I, II, III**
SON OF A DOPE FIEND I II
Renta
GORILLAZ IN THE BAY **I II III IV**
TEARS OF A GANGSTA I II
DE'KARI
TRIGGADALE I II III
Elijah R. Freeman
GOD BLESS THE TRAPPERS I, II, III
THESE SCANDALOUS STREETS I, II, III
FEAR MY GANGSTA I, II, III IV, V
THESE STREETS DON'T LOVE NOBODY I, II
BURY ME A G I, II, III, IV, V
A GANGSTA'S EMPIRE I, II, III, IV
THE DOPEMAN'S BODYGAURD I II
THE REALEST KILLAZ I II
Tranay Adams
THE STREETS ARE CALLING
Duquie Wilson
MARRIED TO A BOSS… I II III
By Destiny Skai & Chris Green
KINGZ OF THE GAME I II III IV

K'ajji

Playa Ray
SLAUGHTER GANG I II III
RUTHLESS HEART I II III
By Willie Slaughter
FUK SHYT
By Blakk Diamond
DON'T F#CK WITH MY HEART I II
By Linnea
ADDICTED TO THE DRAMA I II III
By Jamila
YAYO I II III
A SHOOTER'S AMBITION I II
By S. Allen
TRAP GOD I II
By Troublesome
FOREVER GANGSTA
GLOCKS ON SATIN SHEETS I II
By Adrian Dulan
TOE TAGZ I II III
By Ah'Million
KINGPIN DREAMS I II
By Paper Boi Rari
CONFESSIONS OF A GANGSTA
By Nicholas Lock
I'M NOTHING WITHOUT HIS LOVE
By Monet Dragun
CAUGHT UP IN THE LIFE I II III
By Robert Baptiste
NEW TO THE GAME I II III
By **Malik D. Rice**

LIFE OF A SAVAGE I II III

A GANGSTA'S QUR'AN

MURDA SEASON

GANGLAND CARTEL

By **Romell Tukes**

LOYALTY AIN'T PROMISED

By Keith Williams

QUIET MONEY I II

THUG LIFE

By **Trai'Quan**

THE STREETS MADE ME I II

By **Larry D. Wright**

THE ULTIMATE SACRIFICE I, II, III, IV, V

KHADIFI

IF YOU CROSS ME ONCE

ANGEL I II

By **Anthony Fields**

THE LIFE OF A HOOD STAR

By Ca$h & Rashia Wilson

THE STREETS WILL NEVER CLOSE

By K'ajji

BOOKS BY LDP'S CEO, CA$H

TRUST IN NO MAN

TRUST IN NO MAN 2

TRUST IN NO MAN 3

BONDED BY BLOOD

SHORTY GOT A THUG

THUGS CRY

THUGS CRY 2

THUGS CRY 3

TRUST NO BITCH

TRUST NO BITCH 2

TRUST NO BITCH 3

TIL MY CASKET DROPS

RESTRAINING ORDER

RESTRAINING ORDER 2

IN LOVE WITH A CONVICT

LIFE OF A HOOD STAR

Coming Soon

BONDED BY BLOOD 2

BOW DOWN TO MY GANGSTA

The Streets Will Never Close

Printed in the USA
CPSIA information can be obtained
at www.ICGtesting.com
LVHW020252190224
772209LV00008B/432